GW01044854

THE VENICE AFFAIR

Copyright © 2004 by Janet Burns

All rights reserved. No part of this book shall be reproduced or transmitted in any form or by any means, electronic, mechanical, magnetic, photographic including photocopying, recording or by any information storage and retrieval system, without prior written permission of the publisher. No patent liability is assumed with respect to the use of the information contained herein. Although every precaution has been taken in the preparation of this book, the publisher and author assume no responsibility for errors or omissions. Neither is any liability assumed for damages resulting from the use of the information contained herein.

This is a work of fiction. Names, characters, places, and incidents either are the product of the author's imagination or are used fictitiously. Any resemblance to actual events or locales or persons, living or dead, is entirely coincidental.

ISBN 978-0-7414-1866-1

Printed in the United States of America

Published August, 2005

INFINITY PUBLISHING

Toll-free (877) BUY BOOK
Local Phone (610) 941-9999
Fax (610) 941-9959
Info@buybooksontheweb.com
www.buybooksontheweb.com

Dedication

Dedicated to my daughter, Kira Kathlene Burns,
who has always been the source of my
inspiration, in life and art.

Prologue

What was she doing? Did she really even know? This was crazy. She was out of her mind, no doubt about it. As the airplane soared to its destination she recalled all the times she'd intended to go on a long trip. How she'd always wanted to travel, but never had the time or funds to do so. She didn't really have them now either, but this was an emergency.

Her brother was in trouble. He was in need of her. Ivory smiled to herself as she saw her brother's face in her mind's eye. Maxwell Lawrence was quite all right.

He was always in one situation or another. He was a freelance writer and his profession took him all over, and he always had one incredible story or another to tell her when he returned to Los Angeles.

The Lawrence siblings inherited their coal black hair and green eyes from their mother. Ivory and Maxwell's parents had died in a plane crash almost ten years before. In fact, it had taken Ivory a long time to step aboard the plane. She had always managed to find alternative modes of transportation for her local traveling.

But not this time. Flying was the only way to get to her destination as soon as possible. So she'd very reluctantly boarded the plane at LAX and made it to Newark, New Jersey, with nothing fatal happening. Once aboard the Alitalia flight she was able to breathe easier, and actually believed she would be okay. The worst had been the first twenty minutes after take off in LA. She knew everything would be okay now. She convinced herself of this. At least she hoped so.

Max had been in some kind of an automobile accident. The details had been very vague when he'd told her about it on the telephone. He'd been rather abrupt, not elaborating or answering her questions directly. What he'd basically said was that he'd been in an accident, that he had just been released from the hospital, and could she come right away? He needed her. When she'd asked him what had happened he told her he'd explain later. That he had another problem that only she could help him with and he needed her to come right away and not worry about finances, that he'd pay for everything.

Then he'd hung up. All she knew was that she had to get to him and see for herself how he was. He's said he was fine, but Max always said that. He'd say that if he were stranded in the middle of the Sahara with a dead camel. So Ivory had asked her boss for a leave of absence. It was easily arranged since the engineering company where she worked as a secretary, was in the process of moving to New York. Ivory wouldn't be going with them, although she was asked. She had a house in Redondo Beach that was finally paid off and she couldn't possibly move to New York.

So when she walked out of the office that day it was understood that she probably wouldn't be coming back since the move would be completed in a couple of days and she had no idea how long she'd be gone. Everything had changed. Her brother needed her. So here she was, on her way to Venice, Italy. What had Max been doing in Venice? Another novel? And why had he sounded so odd on the phone the day before? As if he was upset or nervous, maybe even a little scared. But she'd never known Max to be afraid of anything.

She gripped both sides of her seat as a thought came to her. What if he was acting odd because something was physically wrong with him? She mustn't think that way. Surely Max would have told her if there were something seriously wrong with him. Besides, he's said he was at his hotel now. The doctor wouldn't have let him go if his injuries were serious. As the plane started to descend she gripped the armrests.

"I'm coming, Max. I'm coming."

Chapter One

The cool afternoon breeze hit Ivory the minute she stepped off the plane in Italy. As she stood looking around her, she became aware of holding up the line. But when she turned to apologize she saw that the people behind her were doing the same thing. There were two things she noticed first: the historical architecture of the buildings and the water. She actually wasn't yet in Venice itself. She had to cross the water first to get to the town.

So after getting directions and exchanging her American dollars for Lira, she took the motorized bus-boat called the vaporetti to downtown Venice. Ivory was speechless as she looked at everything around her. Venice was a bustling place, but not too crowded for late September. The buildings. Oh, what magnificent buildings. She had to take some time while she was there to see the sights. Perhaps Max would take her.

Passengers were to disembark at the dock near their destination, and one had to be very careful when one got off the vaporetti. Fortunately she'd bought a map at the airport and finding her brother's hotel was very easy. Everyone was friendly and willing to direct her to the Hotel Albergo Guerrato. A colorful produce market stood next to the hotel and she could glimpse the Rialto Bridge from where she stood. The hotel was very old. She was surprised to meet the owners themselves. They spoke perfect English.

As Mrs. Piero showed her the way to her brother's room, the middle-aged woman told her that the hotel was 800 years old. Ivory thought it had an old- world quality to it, very airy and decorated with antiques as well as modern art. Max had a corner room upstairs. Mrs. Piero knew about his accident and told her she hoped he recovered soon. He was such a nice and charming man. Ivory almost asked her about the accident, but thought it inappropriate.

She would soon find out anyway. After thanking Mrs.

Piero she knocked on the door and almost immediately she heard Max say 'Come in.' When she walked into the elaborately antique-decorated room she saw Max lying on a four poster bed to the right. The left side was a sitting room with sofa, a couple of chairs and tables.

"Sis! You came!"

She looked at him and then closed the door behind her.

"Of course I came. You sounded very odd over the phone."

She went to his bedside and bent down to kiss him on the forehead, as she looked him over critically. As usual, a lock of black hair fell forward over his forehead and she noticed that he'd grown his hair longer. He was such a handsome man. Max was thirty years old, three years younger than she was, but he acted much younger.

To her, Max would always be that little boy she had to protect and take care of. He didn't need her protection now, of course. He was a grown man with a good job. It didn't look as though he had shaved in days, but the result was that he looked rugged and earthy. He was still wearing a hospital gown of green and it fell off one shoulder. His muscled arms fairly bulged with biceps and not for the first time, she marveled at what a beautiful man he was. Beautiful and kind. At least he had always been kind to her.

She'd heard him snap at quite a few people before, but his irritation was hardly ever aimed at her. Theirs was a warm and special relationship. She was the one who sometimes got exasperated with him. Almost identical green eyes looked up at her and immediately a boyish grin spread across his face as he exclaimed, "I can't believe you're here so soon!"

She pulled up a chair as her gaze traveled over him.

"You don't look seriously injured, thank God."

He pushed down the blanket that had been covering him and she saw that his left leg was in a cast up to the knee and his right wrist was bandaged. The he lifted the top of the hospital shirt and she gasped when she saw the bandages around his waist. He was quick to say, "Hold on, sis. A few ribs were broken, that's all."

"That's all? What the hell happened? Look at you!"

She plopped down on the chair she'd almost forgotten about and he said, "I'll tell you everything, but I want to start at the beginning because there's something I want you to do for me."

She looked at him inquiringly. He pulled the blanket back up and began; "I was on my way to Palazzo Delegado when this car came out of nowhere and hit me from the side. I never saw it. I was instantly knocked unconscious and the next thing I knew I was in a hospital, waking up with these bandages around my waist. They fixed me up but told me I had to stay in bed for several weeks to give my body a chance to heal."

"But your face looks fine. No scratches or anything."

"I was lucky."

"Not so lucky."

"It was a hit and run apparently. It was late at night and no witnesses stepped forward. Anyway, I'm fine now. This happened three days ago. I called you as soon as I could. I've been heavily sedated."

Ivory studied him for a moment and then asked, "Who was at this Palazzo Delegado?"

"Victoria Ashford, the famous actress. You may have heard of her. She was popular in the fifties. But after a few films she disappeared. The story goes she moved to Venice, never to be seen or heard from again in Hollywood."

"I know how the story goes, Max."

"You do?"

He looked surprised. She informed him, "I don't know where or when I heard about her, but I know the story from somewhere."

"Anyway, I was on my way to interview her. I thought her life would make a good novel. Fiction, of course. The names would be changed."

"And where does Ms. Ashford live?"

"Here in Venice, in the Dorsoduro section. That's right off Canal Della Guidecca, on the west end."

Ivory got up and started walking around. "I see."

Max relaxed against the pillows and went on, "Anyhow, what I want to ask you is if you'll go in my place. Obviously I can't go in my condition. I'll have to stay put. All you have to do is go, take a look around, and talk with Ms. Ashford. But don't let the rest of the family know. She asked for complete secrecy. You can do this, Ivory. You used to write. I know it was a long time ago. I have a friend who's a photographer who will be going with you. He can help you. He already knows what's happened to me. You two will go as her guests."

Ivory went to the window and looked out at the view. She could see the Rialto Bridge clearly from there.

"Guests? How would she have met us if she's been secluded for all these years? I heard somewhere that she has been secluded."

Max was quiet for a minute. Then he sighed. "We haven't exactly worked all this out yet."

"I'll say you haven't."

She turned to him and said as she walked back over to the bed, "Apparently you haven't been thinking too clearly, brother dear."

Her tone had been sharp so Max looked at her, a little puzzled. "What do you mean by that, sis?"

She put her hands on her hips and snapped, "Don't you 'sis' me! Whatever gave you the idea that I'd just go along with this! You must've been delirious when you invented this preposterous story!"

"Why are you upset? What are you saying?"

"I'm saying, Maxwell Lawrence, that you are lying! You're lying to me and I want to know why!"

Max looked taken back and shocked. Ivory returned to the chair next to the bed and took a deep breath before saying, "All right, Max, tell me what's really going on."

He looked away. "I don't know what you mean."

"Sure you do, babe. You're lying to me about your accident, and God only knows what else."

He just looked at her. "Why do you think that?"

She smiled. "You mean, what gave you away?"

Max became frustrated and angry, as he snapped, "No, I mean what in the hell are you talking about!"

She laughed. "Very good, Maxwell. Indignation and anger. You play your part very well, but I'm afraid it won't work with me."

"Damn it, Ivory! What are you talking about?"

Her gaze narrowed and Max began to get nervous. He couldn't remember a time when she'd looked at him quite like that. At least not since they were kids. She spoke in a calm, collected tone; "I'm talking about you lying to me about this accident you were in."

Her voice changed then and she wasn't so calm. "This is Venice, you idiot! There are no cars here! Water surrounds us everywhere, and since you said you were on your way to Palazzo Delegado, which is also here in Venice, a car couldn't possibly have run you down. And before you start telling me some story about being somewhere else in Italy when you were hit, save your breath.

Because if you were hit somewhere else, you wouldn't be transported to this hotel, not in your condition. Besides, you already told me you were here, on your way to the palazzo, and I can always tell when you're lying, Maxwell!"

To say that several expressions flashed across Max's face would've been an understatement. Finally he heaved a sigh. "Okay, okay. I should've known you'd figure this out. I forgot about there being no cars. I was pretty drugged when I called you. I guess I just said the first thing that popped into my head. Sorry, sis."

"Why did you lie to me? What really happened?"

"I was beat up. Coming out of a nightclub one night I was jumped and dragged into an alley. Two guys, I think, and one of them warned me to mind my own business. I didn't want to tell you the truth because I knew you'd worry about me and tell me to forget all about this. But I can't, Ivory. It isn't just the story I'm after."

"What are you after, Max? And why do you want me to go to the Palazzo? It's apparently dangerous. I'm assuming they were warning you about the interview with Victoria Ashford. Someone doesn't want you there and they won't want me there either."

"That's why you're to go in secrecy. Someone obviously found out who I am. No one knows who you are. But there's more. This isn't about me and my interview."

"What do you mean? What is it about? Who else is involved?"

"A friend of mine," replied Max, "A good friend of mine. This is all about him. What I told you about getting the story, this research on Victoria Ashford, is only a small part of it. That isn't the real reason I wanted to go to palazzo Delegado."

"I think you better explain, Max," she told him.

He tried to smile at her and then said, "This is about Tyler. Tyler Scott Ashford."

Ivory just looked at him in silence for a few minutes. "Who?"

"Tyler Ashford."

"Wait a minute. This is your friend, the photographer?"

"Yes."

"He's related to Victoria?"

"Right. He's her grandson."

"What's this all about, Max?"

"Okay. Just listen, will you? Hear me out before jumping to any conclusions. I met Tyler a long time ago. About seven or eight years ago. I got in a sticky situation in Morocco and he helped me out. In fact, he saved my life. That was when I wrote that article about customs and society in Morocco. Well, I got mixed up with the wrong kind of characters and I met Tyler in a bar one night. We got acquainted and started hanging out together.

He warned me about certain people. You see, I was seeing this woman named Layla and I had no idea she was married. Her husband found out and sent some guys after me one night. They were beating me up pretty good, they were huge men, mind you, and Tyler came from out of nowhere and took care of them. Together we fought them off. One of them was about to stab me when Tyler kicked the knife out of his hand."

"My God, Max!"

"Yeah, it was pretty bad. But the worst of it was yet to come. Layla's husband had her murdered and tried to pin the murder on me. He had a friend of his, a bartender, tell the police he saw Layla and I leave the bar together and that we were arguing. As it happened, she was killed the same night Tyler and I had the fight with his men. They threw me in jail and I thought I was already dead. Then Tyler came in and talked to the authorities. They knew him, you see.

I don't know what he was doing in Morocco, but he told them I was with him all night and on his word alone they released me within the hour. What I told you was true. Tyler is a photographer, but he's also somewhat of a mystery. I know he has several businesses. I never knew what he was doing in Morocco, all I knew was that he saved my life."

Ivory exclaimed, "You could've been killed, Max! One way or another! Why didn't you tell me about this before?"

He took her hand in his and replied, "I didn't want to worry you. Besides, I was rather ashamed of my conduct. I want you to know that I've tried to be more careful since then. Especially in a foreign country."

"But what about now, Max? You were attacked a few days ago and put in the hospital. This sounds dangerous to me."

Max leaned over and grabbed his cigarettes. As he lit one he said, "This is different, sis. This is for Tyler. I owe him."

He inhaled and exhaled and then went on, "Last week I was in Miami just finishing up an article I was writing for an outdoors magazine, all about fishing, if you can believe that, when Tyler e-mailed me and asked to see me. We met in Fort Lauderdale for lunch and he asked for my help.

When Tyler was a boy he used to live with his parents and his grandmother in Venice after Victoria left Hollywood. She chose Venice because the family has a palazzo here. I

7

don't know all the details, but after Tyler's father died of a heart attack, his mother left Venice, leaving Ty with his grandmother when he was seven. Victoria was Tyler's father's mother. He didn't really elaborate and I got the feeling he doesn't like to talk about it.

When Tyler was ten he was sent away to school and he never went back. He's concerned now because he read in a Venetian newspaper recently that his aunt, who has lived with Victoria for many years, was found murdered two weeks ago. The poor woman was strangled. A maid found her in the tower room in the west wing."

Chapter Two

"Strangled! My God! What have you gotten yourself involved in?"

Max didn't say anything; he just looked kind of helpless for a minute or so. Ivory frowned. "There's something I don't understand. You asked me to go to the palazzo and get the story on Victoria. Why?"

"Well, it's like this. Tyler and I were going to go to the palazzo on the pretext of writing her story. I already had her permission to do so, but she thought it wise to say that we were friends of a friend. As I said, we haven't worked out the details. But Ty just wants to see for himself if his grandmother is all right. He wasn't going to let on who he was and since none of the family have seen him since he was very young, they wouldn't recognize him."

"But why does he want to go as someone else? Why not just go for a visit and see for himself?"

Max hesitated and then answered her question, "He thinks something is going on there. After all, a woman was murdered. Maybe he thinks he could find out more as a photographer or an acquaintance."

"But why would Victoria agree to see you? As you said, there was a murder committed there. Hardly the time for company.

"Tyler is going by the name of Scotty Theodore. You see, it's a message to his grandmother. When he was young she used to occasionally call him Scotty. And the last name he's using is the name of a stuffed bear he had as a child. He's telling his grandmother that he wants to see her and that he wants no one else to know. And apparently she got the message because I received a reply from her the next day, granting permission."

"But then you were attacked by two men."

"Yes. Someone found out and didn't want me to go to the palazzo."

"Perhaps they didn't want the publicity that might occur from your visit."

"You got it. So then the plan was to ask you to go in my place. Tyler doesn't like that plan. We've been communicating by phone and e-mail since the accident. He had some business in New York to see to. He doesn't want you involved at all because of what happened to me."

"But you were going to involve me anyway. And how can I succeed where you have failed?"

He shrugged his shoulders. Then she asked, "Shouldn't you have formulated a new plan before you involved me?"

He nodded. "Yes, but I didn't think you'd be here so soon. I thought it would be a couple of days before you could get away. Because of your job and all."

"I no longer have that particular job."

"What?"

"Mr. Forester is relocating. Never mind. Let's get back to the problem at hand."

"So you're free?" asked Max, "You don't have to get back right away?"

"That's right. So where do we go from here?"

"I don't know. I sent a message to Ms. Ashford, explaining I was in an accident. I fell down the stairs and broke my leg and fractured my hip."

Ivory stood up. "Great! You tell her a believable story, but you tell me an unbelievable one!"

Max grinned. "That's only because I was thinking clearer this morning when I sent the message. I'd already made my mistake with you on the phone."

She started pacing. "Don't ever lie to me again, Maxwell. Did you think I wouldn't help you?"

Max hesitated and then asked in a surprised tone, "You mean you will help?"

She went to the window and looked out again. It was such a lovely day. She should be enjoying the scenery and seeing the sights. Instead she was here with Max, in his condition, planning a way to get into a place where she'd be in danger of one kind or another, and doing it all for a man she'd never even met. She turned around to look at her brother.

"I don't know, Max. This whole thing is so bizarre. Right now I'm going to go get a room and order a late lunch. I'm really tired and I need a nap."

"I've already arranged a room for you. It's right next door."

He picked up a key from the nightstand and held it out to her. She took it from him as she tried to smile. "Thanks, Max."

"You're welcome, sis. Your luggage should already be in the room."

She went towards the door. "There was a problem with my luggage at the airport and I didn't want to hang around and wait."

"What kind of problem?"

"They were backed up or something. Some incident had occurred, I don't know. They said they'd send it later. Maybe they lost it."

"Misplaced, more likely. I'll have Mrs. Piero check on it."

"Thanks."

She opened the door. "I'll see you later."

"Ivory?"

She turned to him. He spoke sincerely, "I'm really sorry I dragged you into all of this. I'm also sorry I lied to you."

She smiled. "Forget it. You were trying to help a friend."

"True, but you're my sister. I should've known you'd understand. I also should've known you'd be able to tell I was lying."

"Yes, you should've."

She closed the door then and went to her own room.

After Ivory woke from her nap she stretched languorously and looked around her at the lovely and quaint room. She was lying on an oak, canopied bed with pink gauze hangings and a pink and white patchwork quilt. The rest of the furnishings were antique also. A matching dresser and vanity. On the other end of the pink and white striped wallpapered room, was a Victorian settee and Queen Anne chair. Over the settee were two large Venetian windows with the same pink gauze covering them. It was now dark outside.

This could've been her dream vacation. She sat up when there was a knock on the door. She called for them to enter and a young man came in with her two suitcases. He looked to be in his late twenties. He smiled broadly and said, "Buon Giorno."

She had an Italian phrase book but didn't need it for this greeting. She smiled. "Grazie."

He left and she got up to unpack. After putting her clothes away, she went into the bathroom and after a hot shower, changed into a long purple flowered dress and brushed out her shoulder-length black hair.

After pinning it up she left the room and went to knock on Max's door. When there was no answer she opened it and looked in. He was sound asleep. She noticed the bottle of prescription pills on his nightstand. She closed the door and went down the wide carpeted staircase to the floor below.

To her right was the office. The same young man who had brought her luggage stood behind the counter, writing in a book. She smiled at him and said, "Buon Giorno."

He looked up and smiled also. She tried her Italian. "Dove'e' un ristorante?"

She was hungry. Certainly he could help her find a restaurant. He stepped out from behind the counter and pointed to a door to the left. "Un ristorante."

She told him 'Grazie' and went to the door. He said, "Arrividerci." behind her.

She turned to smile at him but he was gone. The restaurant was just as quaint as the rest of the Inn. She was seated at a small round table with a red and white checkered tablecloth covering it. Ivory totally enjoyed her meal of fried mozzarella cheese, calamari, piatto misto and wine.

Afterwards, she checked on her brother again but he was still asleep, so she decided to go for a walk. The night was cool but she was rather warm, so she took no sweater. Venice at night was just as interesting as Venice by day. Maybe even more so because she loved the night. She glimpsed gondolas on the shimmering water and decided to take a ride in one of them very soon.

But not tonight. Tonight she wanted to walk, and walk she did. She passed a huge post office with a postal boat moored at its blue posts. It was to the left of the Rialto Bridge. The bridge was a symbol of Venice, she knew, and the area was lined with shops as well as tourists. She'd read a lot about Venice on her flight over. The Rialto Bridge had been built in 1592. Locals called the summit of the bridge the 'Icebox of Venice' because of its cool breeze.

She wrapped her arms about herself as the night air hit her. Rialto meant 'High River'. There were restaurants lining the canal beyond the bridge, as well. The Rialto section had been a separate town in the early days, known for its commercialization. The San Marco district was the religious and government center. A street called 'Merceria' connected the two, offering tourists many shopping temptations.

But she didn't feel like shopping. All she wanted to do was clear her head. She remembered reading that through the 14th and 15th centuries, German pilgrims had stayed in the Rialto district on their way to the Holy Land. They thought it was the most popular area and the Inn of St. George was the most popular Inn.

The map of Venice by Jacopo de' Barbari, which was located in the Correr Museum, shows the inn standing beside the Fondaco dei Tedeshci, which now housed the post office. There was so much to explore, but the hour was rather late and the three glasses of wine she'd had with dinner were beginning to make her very sleepy. She'd have to explore the rest of Venice some other time.

Chapter Three

Ivory was still sleeping when the telephone rang beside her bed. At first she was disoriented. She sat up and rubbed her eyes while reaching for the phone. No one should be woken first thing in the morning by a persistent telephone. There ought to be a law against it. "Yes? What is it?"

"Good morning, sunshine," Max said cheerfully. Ivory groaned and he laughed. "I guess you were still sleeping, huh?"

"You guessed right, Einstein."

"Still not a morning person, eh?"

"Is there something you wanted, Max, or are you just trying to be irritating?"

"Okay, sis. Of course I'm calling for a reason. I received a message from Ms. Ashford this morning."

"Obviously she's a morning person also."

"That's right. I waited an hour before I called you."

"Good grief. What time is it?"

"Seven-thirty. I received the message at six."

"Great. All of Venice gets up at the crack of dawn."

"Of course. I've already had my breakfast."

"Good for you. So do you mind if I have mine before I come to your room?"

"Not at all," Max replied patiently, "Take your time."

"I intend to."

She hung up the phone and plopped back on the bed. It had taken her quite awhile to get to sleep the night before. She'd tossed and turned while thinking about everything that Max had told her. Around two in the morning she'd finally come to the conclusion that she only had one choice; to help Max and his friend.

Dangerous or not, she had to at least hear what sort of plan they came up with. After all, this Tyler person had saved her brother's life. When Max had gotten into trouble, he hadn't had to get involved. But he had and Max had gotten out of what would have been a horrible jail and he'd also cleared him of murder. It was really all so incredible. But it had really happened and she knew Max always repaid his debts. But this was a huge pay off. Regardless, she had to help her brother. And she had to help Tyler Ashford as well.

About an hour later, Ivory walked into her brother's room. He was sitting up in bed, reading. He put the book down as he took in his sister's appearance. She was as beautiful as ever. She wore a white cotton dress that flowed around her calves and her hair was up in some kind of arrangement. Once again, he had to wonder why this woman wasn't married yet.

Were all the men she knew complete idiots? Wait until Ty saw her. His friend had had several girlfriends, but nothing serious that he knew of. Tyler was a loner, an enigma, and he'd never actually seen him with a woman. But whenever they'd been together they both had appreciated certain women's looks. Maybe he should worry. Ty could be charming when he wanted to.

But he knew his sister. She could take care of herself. And she didn't encourage men's attentions. She'd been burned as he had. Ivory sat down on the chair that still remained by the bed. She smiled. "Is there anything I can get for you or help you with, Max? It must hurt to move."

"It does, which is why I move very slowly."

She laughed. He added, "But I don't need you to do a thing, sis. The fact that you're here is all I need. How was your night?"

"Fine. I took a walk after dinner. But I had a hard time getting to sleep."

"Why?"

"I think you know the answer to that."

He sobered. "You were thinking about what I told you. Of course you were. And did you come up with any conclusions or revelations?"

"I guess that all depends on you and your friend, now doesn't it? However, I will tell you that I would like to help, Maxwell. If you want to help your friend, then so do I."

He smiled warmly at her. "What would I do without you, Ivory? Life would be so dull."

"I don't think your life could ever be dull, brother dear. Just look at the situation you're in now."

"Yes, but this isn't exactly my situation."

"Right. It's Tyler Ashfords'."

"Ty is a great guy, sis. I'm sure you two will hit it off."

She frowned. "Listen, Max, I'm not here to hit it off with anyone. I'm here to help you, and only that."

"Jeez, Ivory. Take it easy. Just take a deep breath. Don't get so serious on me. Try to lighten up, have a little fun."

"Having fun is what gets you into most of your situations. How can I have fun when my brother is laid up from a beating he took from some thugs? This is serious business, Max."

"You don't have to tell me how serious it is!" Max shot back, "After all, I'm the one lying in this damn bed!"

Ivory just looked at him and said nothing. He turned to pick up his coffee cup. After a sip he put it down with a bang. Ivory sighed. "I'm sorry, Max. I'm sure it isn't easy lying in bed all the time."

"No, it isn't, and to make matters worse, I can't do a damn thing to help Ty. I have to ask you to do it. Do you think I like being in this position?"

"No, I guess not. But we can't do anything about it. What's done is done, Max. Now we have to think about what to do next. What did Victoria say in her message?"

Max leaned back on the pillow and smoothed the bed covers over his chest. "It isn't good news. She said it won't be possible to have an interview at this time since the family is grieving for her sister."

"That's all she said?"

"Afraid so."

"So now what?"

"Beats me. I've been trying to get a hold of Tyler. He doesn't answer his phone or respond to the e-mails I've sent. All I can do is keep trying. I know he planned on coming here after his business was concluded."

"Well, what else is there to really do? No visitors will be allowed at the palazzo. And with good reason. A murder was just committed there."

"Well, we'll see what Ty has to say."

"What can he say, Max? You might not be able to help him with this. Certainly there has to be another way he can find out about his grandmother."

"Maybe. There's something else I want to talk to you about. It seems there is something you can do for me."

"What?"

"There's going to be a party here tonight. They have a small ballroom at the back of the inn and there's going to be a Masquerade Ball there this evening in honor of Mr. and Mrs. Piero's anniversary. Their 50th anniversary. The doctor gave me crutches to start walking with, but I don't think I'm up to it yet. I really don't think I will be able to attend, so will you go in my place?"

Ivory hesitated. A Masquerade Ball. She'd always wanted to dress up and go to one but the opportunity never presented itself. And here she was in Venice where Masquerade Balls were an occasional occurrence. She looked at her brother. He was waiting for a reply. She stood up. "I can't go to a Masquerade Ball, Max."

"And why not?"

"Well, for one thing, I have nothing to wear. And I wouldn't feel right leaving you here while I go to some party."

"Ivory, this town is full of costume shops and you have all day to pick out a costume. Here."

He tossed her something. When she caught it she saw that it was a credit card. She said, "I am capable of paying for my own costume, Max."

"I don't want you paying for it. I want to do this for you. Buy a complete ensemble. Anything you want. I will

17

be quite happy here; knowing you'll be having a good time. I dragged you to Venice. I'm involving you in this mess. So let me do this for you. I need to do this, sis."

He had a pleading look on his face. How could she refuse him? It seemed so important to him. Besides, she wanted to go.

"Well?" he asked, "What do you think?"

"About what? The Masquerade Ball or you paying for my costume?"

"Either one."

"I think I'll take you up on both offers. It may even be fun."

"Of course it will be fun! I bet you haven't gone out and had any fun in a very long time."

"Never mind. I said I'd go. Let's not analyze it to death."

Max laughed. Ivory headed straight for the door. "Where are you going?" he asked.

She turned as she opened the door. "I'm going shopping. You don't think it's easy choosing the perfect costume, do you? I'll probably have to go to several shops before I find the right one. It's not every day I get to go to a Masquerade Ball, you know."

"Okay, okay. I get the point. Be careful and have fun."

She called out, "Yes, Daddy." as she closed the door behind her.

Chapter Four

For the next few hours Ivory was excited, awed, and astounded. There were several costume shops not far from the inn and she found what she was looking for in the third one she walked into. The decision of who to dress up as, was a difficult one. There were several personalities she would like to be. But finally, after much deliberation, she decided to go as Cleopatra, Queen of the Nile.

It took her several hours to choose the costume, have her hair done, as well as her nails. But through it all she remained excited and very happy. Just as she walked into her room with arms full of packages, the phone rang. She dropped everything on the bed and breathlessly answered the phone. It was Max, wondering where she'd been.

He had been a little concerned about her. She laughed at his over-protectiveness and promised to come to his room in her costume when she was ready. There had been no word from Tyler yet. After hanging up with Max, she called and ordered lunch. While waiting for her food to be brought, she went over to the full-length mirror to look at herself.

Her hair was crimped in small waves just as she'd seen Cleopatra's in some movie. Ivory began opening the packages and in the middle of this Mrs. Piero came with her lunch. Mrs. Piero asked Ivory if she would be attending the ball and she was happy to tell her that she was. Mrs. Piero was glad. After hanging up the costume and putting certain things aside, Ivory decided to take a nap. After all, she had a big night ahead of her.

Mrs. Piero came back for the dishes and Ivory thanked her. As she drifted off to sleep she realized she hadn't seen much of her brother that day, but then reminded herself that this had all been his idea in the first place. Anyway, chances were Max and her were finished here. There didn't seem to be any more they could do for Mr. Ashford.

At least she'd have the memory of the Masquerade Ball

to take with her. She didn't regret coming to Venice. Not at all. It was really a beautiful place with always something new to see or experience. She'd had a great day and hadn't felt so relaxed and content in a very long time.

Ivory's 'short' nap turned out to be longer than she'd anticipated. And once again the ringing of the phone woke her. It actually startled her so much that she sprang up into a sitting position as she complained, "That's it! That is it! Either that phone is going or I am!" When she looked out the windows she saw that it was getting dark. "Damn!" and then she snatched up the phone. "Max?"

"Yes?"

"I overslept."

"I figured as much."

"I've got to go. I'm going to be late."

"It's a ball, sister dear, it's okay to be fashionably late."

"I'll be there as soon as I can."

"Okay. I've got a surprise for you."

"For me? What is it?"

"Hel - lo. I said it's a surprise."

"I know, but, oh hell, I can't talk about this anymore. I've got to get ready."

She hung up the phone and then called downstairs for coffee to be sent up. She told them to just leave it on the table in the sitting room. And then she wrapped a towel around her head and got in the shower. Where had the time gone? Maybe it was jet lag or something. Or perhaps it was just very easy to oversleep in Venice.

An hour later Ivory stood before the mirror. She studied her reflection as she held her breath. Was that really her? Of course it was, but there was just such a difference in her appearance. She seemed to be covered in gold. The long tight-fitting gown hugged her body and flowed out just below her knees. Gold heels went with it as well as a smooth gold-fitted breastplate that covered her chest and tapered down to her waist. It gleamed in the light. There was a gold neckband around her throat with a black onyx sphinx dangling from it.

Upon her head was a thin circlet of gold with strands of gold intermingling with her crimped black hair. Doing her make up had been the fun part. Black eyeliner emphasized the cat-like shape of her green eyes. She wore deep red lipstick and a gold bracelet circled her right upper forearm. In fact, she thought she really did look like Cleopatra.

Max was speechless when she walked into his room. And then he whistled and said as he placed his hand over his heart, "Please don't tell me that's you, Ivory. Let me think a goddess has come into my life at last!"

She laughed. "Sorry Max, it's only me. You'll have to find your goddess elsewhere."

"Damn!"

She turned in a circle before him. "You look great!" he exclaimed, "You look like a queen."

"Okay, so what's my surprise?"

"Ah, you remembered."

"Of course I did."

"Okay, your highness. Sit down and close your eyes."

She did and after a few minutes he told her to open them. She watched in awe as he walked towards her from across the room with the aid of crutches. It was slow progress, but he made it. "Max!" she exclaimed, "That's great! Are you in much pain?"

"Yes, unfortunately. But I have something else for you."

He eased himself back on the bed and set the crutches aside as he opened the drawer of his nightstand and pulled out a golden mask. He said, "I bought this my first day here. I thought it might come in handy if I were invited to a Masquerade Ball."

He handed it to her. It was beautiful. The mask was gold with three strands of tiny gold ribbons hanging down from a gold rose at one corner of it.

"I bought a couple of them, actually. The other one is black with sequins, but this one seems to go with your outfit perfectly. It doesn't take ones attention from that gold circlet you're wearing on your head. You really look great, Ivory."

"Thanks. And thank you for the lovely mask. I can't believe I forgot to buy one. In fact, thanks for everything."

"You're welcome, now put on your mask and get out of here."

"But what about you?" she asked in a concerned tone, "Are you okay?"

"Yes, but I think I need to rest. I've been practicing for a little while now."

"Well, lay down. Have you had dinner?"

"It's on its way. Mrs. Piero's nephew is bringing it up."

"Oh? Is that the Italian young man I saw before?"

"Probably. He helps them out every few days or so. Now go, Ivory. Your subjects are waiting."

Chapter Five

The ballroom was an incredible sight. It was located just past the dining room and double doors stood open to the festivities. Music poured from the room and everyone was dressed in colorful and elaborate costumes. Her mask in place, Ivory went in. Purple and pink balloons and streamers hung from the ceiling and floated on the floor as well as along the walls and in the air itself. The music was from the Venetian age and people were dancing. Along the left wall was a bar where a court jester was serving drinks.

Just inside the door to the right, small tables and chairs were set up. A few people were there, talking animatedly. She saw many costumes she recognized; Marie Antoinette, Queen Elizabeth, several assorted kings, pirates, Biblical characters, vampires, Renaissance clowns, and several others that she didn't recognize.

"Ms. Lawrence?"

Ivory turned and Joan of Arc was standing in front of her. Mrs. Piero removed her mask and introduced her husband, who was Zorro. "Thank you for coming, Ms. Lawrence. Too bad your brother couldn't be here."

"Please, call me Ivory. And actually, Max was walking with the help of crutches earlier. He's resting now."

"Oh really? How wonderful. But he must have been in pain."

"He was. I guess its part of the healing process."

Zorro excused himself and wandered off. Mrs. Piero watched him and then said, "My husband isn't very sociable, I'm afraid. He's a bit of a loner. He's happier in his little office working on his accounts."

"I understand completely, Mrs. Piero."

"My dear, call me Greta. And what a pretty name you have."

"Thank you. This is quite a party."

"Yes, it turned out rather well, I think. Have you met

anyone yet?"

"No, I just arrived."

Greta signaled to someone across the room and a man came over to them. He was Zeus, by the looks of him. Tall and thin with dark curly hair. When he removed the silver mask, Ivory saw that he was Italian. "This is my nephew, Antonio. Antonio, this is Ms. Lawrence. She and her brother Maxwell are guests here."

Antonio bowed deeply and said in perfect English, "An honor, Ms. Lawrence."

Ivory smiled and shook his hand. She too lowered her mask and for a moment Antonio just looked at her, smiling. Ivory turned to Greta. "You have another nephew who works here sometimes, don't you?"

"Si'. He's here somewhere. His name is Dominic. Excuse me, won't you?"

Ivory nodded and Greta walked away, leaving the two of them alone. Antonio asked, "Would you care for something to drink, Ms. Lawrence?"

She smiled. "Yes, I would, actually."

He led her over to the bar and once he ordered them champagne, she looked at the handsome Antonio and asked, "Tell me, how is it that you speak English so well?"

"You mean because my little brother speaks only Italian?"

She nodded. He handed her the champagne. "I was raised in London. Dominic was raised here. Different mothers, you see."

"I do see."

"How about you, Ms. Lawrence? Where are you from?"

"Los Angeles."

"You are a long way from home. How are you enjoying Venice?"

"I'm enjoying it very much. This is a beautiful city."

"Yes, Venice is beautiful, and you are enchanting."

She was taken back momentarily. He was smiling at her. She returned the smile. "It's the costume."

"I think not. I think you must be enchanting whether

24

you're dressed as Cleopatra or not."

Ivory didn't know quite how to respond. She'd been out of circulation far too long, she supposed. But was any woman ready for Antonio and his disarming smile? She turned to gaze out at the costumed dancers. Everyone seemed to be having a good time. Across the room a man dressed as a Viking caught her eye.

That was probably because he was looking right at her. He was casually leaning against the far wall with a drink in his gloved hand. This rather tall and muscular Viking wore no mask. His costume fit him perfectly. He wore a brown velvet tunic with a black leather belt wrapped around his waist. His leggings were black with sheepskin boots that went up to his knees.

Around his neck was a silver chain and at the end of it was a round silver amulet. On the left side of his belt hung a scabbard with a sword encased in it. The sword hilt was encrusted with jewels of some kind. On his head was a Viking helmet and light blonde hair streamed down to his shoulders.

His features were somewhat chiseled but even from that distance she could see that he was a breathtakingly handsome man. The Viking wasn't smiling at her, but simply staring at her with a penetrating gaze. Muscled arms completed his costume and he had his other hand resting on the hilt of his sword. If she hadn't known differently, she would swear he was the real thing. That a Viking lord had somehow materialized out of the past.

"Would you care to dance?" asked Antonio, startling her.

She turned to smile at him and nod. Leaving her drink on the bar after taking one last sip, she let Antonio lead her amongst the other dancers. Antonio was a superb dancer and he held her lightly. After a few minutes she looked for the Viking again, but he was gone. Perhaps she'd imagined him. No, that penetrating stare of his had been real enough. She danced with Antonio a couple of times and also with a pirate and a court jester.

She was given another glass of champagne and decided some fresh air would be nice. Next to the bar was a door leading outside. She went out the door and found herself on a rather large balcony that ran the length of the building. No one was out on the balcony that she could see. Shrubbery grew along the railing in places as well as sweet smelling blossoms.

She went to the railing and gazed down at Venice below her. Such a beautiful sight. So colorful, and the water surrounding it glistened from the full moon above. She inhaled deeply and set her mask aside on a table next to the railing. She was quite a distance from the ballroom.

The balcony was a good ten feet in width. The music was not as loud here and Ivory found it quite peaceful. Who would've thought she would ever have attended a Masquerade Ball in Venice dressed up as the Queen of Egypt? And she was enjoying every moment of it.

"Good evening, your highness."

The deep masculine voice made her jump and she turned to its owner. The Viking stood directly behind her. There was adequate lighting on the balcony so she could see him clearly. Now she saw that he had blue eyes and was even more impressive up close. "You startled me."

"Cleopatra, startled? I think not."

He smiled at her then and she knew without a doubt that this had to be one of the most attractive men she'd ever seen. He went to the rail and gripped it with his hands as he too looked down upon the city. Ivory joined him in the view. "I think even queens are allowed to be startled every now and then."

He turned his head to look at her, lifting one of his brows. He was American, or so his voice indicated. His blonde hair glistened in the moonlight and she was reminded again that he could've just stepped out of the past. He turned to her, leaning one hand on the railing, "Tell me, your highness, what do people call you?"

"They call me 'your highness'."

He laughed. "I mean, what is your name?"

26

"You know my name. It's Cleopatra."

"Yes and I'm Thor, the Viking god. But what is your real name?"

She turned back to the view as she replied, "This is a Masquerade Ball. Tonight I am Cleopatra, and you are Thor."

He stared at her for the longest time. She looked over at him. "Why are you staring?"

"Just admiring your costume. Especially your. . . . ah. . . . breastplate."

She laughed then. "Why thank you. I'll take that as a compliment, coming from a god and all."

"As well you should."

"Tell me, wherever did you get that wig?"

"Why? Do you like it?"

"Yes. It's beautiful."

"So is yours."

"But mine is real."

He looked at her hair for a moment and then said, "So is mine."

They looked at each other in silence and then Ivory spoke, "I don't believe you."

"No? Then touch it and see for yourself."

She hesitated and then reached out to run her fingers through his hair as she pulled on it slightly. As she started to withdraw her hand he grabbed her wrist and said, "Tell me, your highness, what exactly happens when a great queen and a god meet?"

He was very close to her now. She could smell his musk scent. She looked directly into his eyes. "I don't know, Thor. What do you think happens?"

His gaze traveled to her mouth and he spoke softly, "I know exactly what happens."

"You do? Then please enlighten me."

"Are you sure you want to know?"

"No, I'm not, but tell me anyway. Tell what happens when a god and a queen meet."

"This."

He pulled her roughly into his arms and his arm held her tightly about her waist as he lowered his mouth to hers in a searing kiss. She was so shocked she just stood there. He released her mouth and spoke huskily as he gazed into her eyes, "Never tempt the gods, Cleo."

Then he kissed her again but this kiss was different. His lips moved gently over hers in a searching manner. Ivory couldn't remember ever being kissed like this. Maybe it was the champagne or the magical quality of the evening, but she found herself responding to his kiss.

For some reason she felt as though she were drowning and that somehow none of it was real. She put her hands on his chest and he held her closer as the kiss deepened. As their tongues met in a frenzied dance, Ivory began to feel a little lightheaded.

Compared to the way this man was kissing her, she'd never truly been kissed before. Somewhere in the back of her mind she tried to tell herself that she shouldn't be doing this. She shouldn't be kissing a complete stranger and that she hadn't let a man so much as touch her in years, and that this was crazy and she should pull away.

But his arms felt good around her and his mouth felt even better. He put a hand through her hair and tipped her head back slightly as he continued to ravage her mouth. Ivory felt as though she were dreaming. She'd read about kisses like this in romance novels but she never expected to experience such a kiss. Or for a descending hunger to envelope her this way.

"Ivory?"

They broke apart at the sound of Max's voice, but he still held her. Ivory looked over at her brother standing there, leaning on his crutches. Then Max looked at Thor.

"Tyler?"

Ivory gasped and pulled out of her Viking's grasp as she looked at him in shock. "Tyler? As in Tyler Ashford?"

He frowned at her and then at Max. "What's going on, Max? Do you know Cleopatra here?"

Max burst into laughter. "All my life. Cleopatra is my

28

sister."

Ivory and Tyler looked at one another again. Max asked his sister, "Didn't you know who he was, Ivory?"

She shook her head, dumbfounded. Max turned to his friend. "You either?"

"No, of course not."

Max laughed again. Ivory glared at her brother. Then Tyler smiled at her and said, "You should've told me your sister was so beautiful, Max."

"I figured you'd discover that on your own, and apparently you have. Come on you two, this is no place to have this discussion. Let's go up to my room."

The two men started to leave but Ivory remained where she was. Max turned to her. "Coming, sis?"

"No. I'm staying. I'm not ready to leave."

"But Ivory..."

"Go on, Max. I'll be up in a while."

Max turned to go but Tyler was frowning. "A word of advice, Cleopatra. Stay clear of Zeus. He's been hitting on every female here."

She turned back to the railing. "So? What's one more god, more or less?"

He started to say something when Max interrupted him, "Forget it, Ty. She's made up her mind."

"Stubbornness must run in your family."

Ivory waited until they were gone and then took a deep breath. She needed to regain her composure. Tyler Ashford! So that was he. She had been kissing Max's friend. My God, she'd had no idea. This was the man she was supposed to help.

How could she when her heart raced like crazy at the nearness of him? This was impossible! Maybe the allure had simply been too much champagne. Perhaps she had just gotten caught up in the costumes they were wearing and the whole night itself.

"Ms. Lawrence! There you are! I've been looking for you everywhere!"

She turned to face Antonio. He came forward and

smiled at her. "I'm glad you're out here. This gives us a chance to get to know one another better."

She tried to smile back but she was still a little unsettled. Antonio stood before her as he took her hands in his. "You look so lovely in the moonlight."

"Thank you."

"I've wanted to get you alone all night."

Ivory stiffened. "And why is that?"

He laughed. "You must know why. I want to see you again. Perhaps we can have lunch tomorrow."

"Perhaps."

"And perhaps you will allow me to kiss you here under the moonlight?"

She withdrew her hand quickly. "I'm sorry, Antonio. I'm very tired. I was just leaving."

"The party? But I thought we could spend some time together."

"Not tonight."

"Then tomorrow?"

"I don't know. Call me tomorrow. I must go now."

"I'll walk you to your room."

She started walking towards the door quickly. "No need. You stay and enjoy yourself."

Chapter Six

Max and Tyler sat in the sitting area in Max's room. They were having a drink, brandy, and were quiet. Max propped his legs up on the coffee table and winced with the effort. Tyler looked over at him. "Painful?"

"Yes."

"Bad?"

"Off and on."

Max looked over at Tyler where he sat on one of the chairs next to the sofa. "Nice costume, Ty. Looks like you were born a Viking."

"Excuse me," Tyler spoke with a hint of indignation, "but I am not just a mere Viking. I am the God of Vikings. Behold, I am Thor."

Max grinned. "A god, huh? Figures. Of course you would pick a deity instead of a normal-type person."

"Of course."

Max sighed and leaned back on the sofa. "Before Ivory gets here, why don't you tell me where you've been and why I haven't been able to get a hold of you?"

Tyler took a sip of brandy. "I already told you where I was. And you probably couldn't get a hold of me because I was in route coming here. I checked in earlier and thought the ball would be amusing."

"And was it?"

Tyler looked at him over the rim of his glass. "Very."

Max's gaze narrowed as he looked at his friend. Tyler shook his head and said, "Don't give me that look, Max. You needn't concern yourself on your sisters behalf."

"Needn't I?"

"No. She can take care of herself. Besides, I didn't know she was your sister."

"And would it have made a difference?"

Tyler shrugged. Max decided to change the subject. "Why didn't you answer my e-mail?"

"What's with all the questions?" snapped Tyler, "You've never concerned yourself with such things before. I don't check my messages all the time, okay? I pack my laptop away in my suitcase. I'm not one of those stereotypes who have it constantly within reach, including having it on my lap on an airplane. You know I don't like questions about my affairs, Maxwell."

"Well, that's too bad," shot back Max in a clipped tone, "There are going to be a lot of questions, Tyler, and not just from me either. My sister will have quite a few questions, I'm sure, and she's not as tolerant as I've always been! She's agreed to help us and she's entitled to all the information you have. You asked for my help, remember?"

"Damn it, Max! I didn't ask for your sister's help! I don't want her involved in this! I told you that before I met her, and now that I have it's more important than ever not to involve her."

"Why?"

"Because it could be dangerous. Look at what happened to you! Do you really want to put your sister in that kind of jeopardy?"

Max took a drink and then set his glass down on the table next to the sofa. He picked up the pack of cigarettes lying beside the ashtray and lit one as he said matter-of-factly, "It's too late, Ty. I sent for her. She came from LA to help me. I told her our original story and she didn't believe a word of it. I messed up. I told her I got in a car accident.

It didn't take her long to point out that there are no cars in Venice. So I had to tell her the truth. She knows as much as I do. I even told her about Morocco. She will help you because she knows it's what I want."

Tyler was thoughtful for a few minutes. Finally he said, "We could try to change her mind."

Max laughed. "You don't know my sister very well." Tyler looked at him and one of his eyebrows rose. "We could convince her that I've given up on the whole idea."

"I won't lie to her again."

"Do you think I want to? I'm trying to keep her safe."

Max took a drag of his cigarette. "There's another reason I want her in on this."

"What reason is that?"

"I trust her. We need someone we can trust. Whatever plan we come up with, we'll need someone we can trust. More to the point, you need someone you can trust. It isn't a good idea for you to go to the palazzo by yourself. If you'd thought you could do it yourself you would've never contacted me. Besides, I need her to write the story for me. Your grandmother promised me an interview."

"An interview! You were attacked, could've been killed and all you care about is a damn interview! You're willing to put your sister in danger because of your job?"

Now it was Max's turn to get upset. "Just a damn minute, Ty! You know the interview is only part of it! Don't even attempt to know the depth of my feelings for Ivory! She means the world to me! How dare you say such a thing! We're all in this mess because of you!"

Ivory burst into the room at that moment. She shut the door behind her as she said, "I could hear you two down the hall! What's with all the yelling?"

Neither man said anything, just looked away. Max found his burning cigarette suddenly interesting and Tyler was focused on some object across the room. Ivory sat on the vacant chair between them. "Look, you two, I don't have time to play games. I'm very tired, a little tipsy, and my patience has just about run out!"

Tyler looked at her then. Their gazes locked and Max watched them. Such an intense look. He quickly said, "Ty has a problem with you getting involved in this."

Ivory looked at her brother and said irritably, "Well, he should have thought of that before he dragged you into this."

"He didn't drag me into anything!" snapped Max, a little short on patience himself, "I was more than willing to help him. He didn't think twice about helping me and there was quite a lot of risk involved it that, Ivory!"

She smiled. Realization dawned on him then. "You did

that on purpose!"

"Well, it kept you two from yelling at each other, didn't it?"

Max smiled. "I guess it did, at that."

They both looked at Tyler. He shook his head. "Watching you two is just amazing. Are you always like this?"

"Of course." stated Max.

Tyler got up to pour Ivory a brandy. She watched him walk across the room, his sword swinging and his boots making indentations in the carpet. And Max watched her. When Tyler turned around Ivory quickly looked away. Aware of her brother watching her, she looked at him.

"What? Why are you looking at me like that?"

He shook his head. Ivory took the brandy from Tyler and their eyes met. She forced herself to look away from his blue gaze. Max ran a hand through his hair. Once Tyler was seated, Ivory asked her brother, "Did you tell him about the message?"

"What message?" demanded Tyler.

"Your grandmother sent a message this morning," Tyler told him, "It's on the nightstand."

Tyler started to get up but the sword caught in the rug, forcing him back in the chair. Frustrated, he unfastened the belt and the sword and the scabbard fell to the floor. Then he went to read the telegram. Ivory looked at her brother. "How are you feeling, Max?"

"Worn out, I guess."

"You should be in bed. Here, let me help you."

She helped him up and he leaned on her as they made their way to the bed. Once he was lying down, he said, "I'll get ready for bed when we've finished."

"Nonsense. I can help you."

Tyler lowered the telegram and watched as Ivory helped her brother undress. She averted her gaze when he pulled off his pants and pulled on his pajama bottoms. Something close to envy hit him. Not because her attention was centered on Max, but because he'd never had anyone to help him or even to care enough to try.

Once Max was settled back against the pillows, Ivory went to give him a pill from the prescription bottle on the nightstand. She took such care with her brother, smiling at him reassuringly all the while. This told Tyler more about her than words ever could. She was more than just a pretty face. She was kind and caring as well.

He spoke abruptly, "Looks like our bridges are burned here."

Ivory looked over at him. "What are we going to do now?"

"We?"

They studied each other for a moment. Ivory replied determinedly, "Yes, we."

He turned and started to walk around the room. "We have to form another plan. I'm not willing to just let this go. I've been gone too long as it is. I owe my grandmother. I don't care what he says."

Ivory sat down on the chair next to the bed and turned it to face Tyler. "He? Who are you talking about?"

Max looked at Tyler too and waited. Tyler grinned at him. "I guess you were right, Max. It is time to answer questions. Since both of you are determined to get involved in this, I might as well tell you what the real problem is. The reason I'm so concerned about what's happening at the palazzo is because of whom is at the palazzo. His name is Julian Ashford, and he's my uncle."

Ivory and Max just stared at him. Tyler went on, "He came to live with us when I was quite young. Right after both my parents were...gone. He brought his wife and daughter with him. My grandmother was delighted. After all, the palazzo is rather large and she welcomed them with open arms.

The first problems began when I got a little older. Uncle Julian started to change. Oh, not in front of the others. But when he and I were alone I began to notice a change. He was abrupt with me and often cruel physically and mentally. If I did something he didn't like, which was all the time, he'd yell at me and then he started knocking me around sometimes."

He stopped then. It was obvious he didn't want to talk about this. Ivory's heart went out to him. What a horrible thing for a child to endure. He went over to the sofa and sat down as he reached for Max's pack of cigarettes. He laughed a little and said, "I quit smoking over five years ago. Oh well."

He lit up and inhaled deeply. Ivory and Max waited for him to go on. They didn't have long to wait. "Anyway, this went on for awhile. I never told anyone because I didn't think they would believe me. Everyone thought he was good old Uncle Julian. He started handling the family business and his wife Francine became pregnant and had a son whom they named Austin.

Shortly after his birth Julian somehow convinced my grandmother that I should be sent away to school. So I was shipped off to England and I never returned. I wrote my grandmother several times but I never received an answer. Just money in an envelope periodically from my uncle. When I graduated a letter came from my Aunt Abby.

She sent me a few thousand dollars and told me it would be better if I didn't come home. She suggested I start a career, possibly a business. The only reason she gave was that the family was going through a hardship and my uncle was upset. I read between the lines. Uncle Julian didn't want me there, and my grandmother had never written me back so I assumed she agreed with my aunt and uncle.

I was young, hurt, and too proud to confront any of them. I have several businesses now and I ceased to need their money or approval a long time ago. Now that I'm older I realize that my uncle probably kept all my letters from my grandmother. But still, she could've somehow contacted me.

Whatever the reason, we were always close and I didn't understand her abandonment. I still don't. However, that doesn't really matter now. Someone murdered my Aunt Abby and my grandmother could be in danger as well. I don't trust my uncle. Something is going on and I intend to find out what. I haven't thought this all out but I do think the only thing to do now is to go to the palazzo as myself.

By the messages we've received from my grandmother, it appears she does want to see me but her hands are tied now. I wouldn't put it past my uncle to have arranged what happened to you, Max. He doesn't want outsiders at the palazzo. But he isn't going to keep me away any longer."

Ivory looked at Max. He looked tired. The pill was probably making him sleepy. Tyler said as he stubbed out his cigarette, "I don't really feel like talking about this anymore. I hope I didn't bore you with my family history."

Ivory spoke up before Maxwell did, "Don't be ridiculous, Tyler."

It was the first time she'd called him by his name. She smiled at him and he caught his breath. She stood up.

"Max needs to sleep now. We understand why you need to see your grandmother, and we'll help you all we can. Isn't that right, Max?"

But when she looked down at her brother his eyes were closed. He was asleep. She bent down to pull the covers up to his chin. Tyler spoke from behind her, "You love him very much."

She turned to him. "Yes."

He turned away from her and went to retrieve his sword on the floor. "It's really late, Ivory. I'm going to my room now. We'll continue this tomorrow."

He went towards the door without so much as another glance at her. He opened the door and said, "Goodnight." and left without waiting for a response.

After checking to make sure her brother was still asleep, she turned the light out and went to her own room. What a day it had been. So much had happened. She'd met Tyler Ashford and what an experience that had been. After putting away her costume and washing off her make up, she crawled into bed and turned off the light.

She couldn't stop going over in her mind all that Tyler had told them. It was quite a story. She couldn't begin to imagine how she would've handled it. Such a tragic tale.

She felt sympathy for Tyler and truly wanted to help him reunite with his grandmother.

But what could she do? As she finally drifted off to sleep, one thing remained with her regardless of her attempts to push it aside. And that was the memory of Tyler's arms holding her close as he kissed her with a passion and hunger that just for a moment she had felt as well.

Chapter Seven

Ivory woke early the next morning and took a shower. The morning was cool so she decided to wear black knit pants and a red cashmere sweater. Her hair was still crimped so she merely brushed it and left it down. As she put on red lipstick, finishing up her light make up routine, the phone rang. Well, at least this time she hadn't still been sound asleep.

When she picked it up she expected to hear Max's voice, but it was Antonio instead. He wanted to meet her for lunch at one o'clock. She didn't know what the day would bring, so she told him she'd call him before one if she couldn't make it. He said he'd be in the dining room at one and hoped she'd meet him there. After she hung up she left the room.

Antonio. Ivory had no desire to hurt his feelings, but she wasn't interested in anything but friendship. Having lunch with him wasn't exactly committing to anything. It wasn't encouraging him, was it? She'd have to make her feelings perfectly clear to him. That is, if she decided to meet him at all.

Tyler had not yet put in an appearance. Max was alone, dressed and sitting on his already-made bed. He wore jeans that were cut on the side of one leg to accommodate the cast. The shirt he wore was light blue and as usual, contrasted well with his black hair. When Ivory walked in he smiled at her. "Good morning."

"Hi, Max."

"I ordered breakfast for three. It should be here any minute."

She sat at her usual place beside his bed. "You look nice. Well rested and almost like your old self."

"The doctor was here earlier. He changed my bandage.

He seems to think I'm doing fine."

"You are doing fine."

They ate breakfast by themselves since Tyler still hadn't arrived. Ivory needed the time alone with Max. Over their third cup of coffee someone came for the dishes. Max had them take the extra breakfast away as well. He told his sister, "Maybe Ty decided to have his breakfast in the dining room."

"Have you called him?"

"No, I didn't want to rush him. Last night was difficult for Ty. That's the most he's ever talked about himself. What do you think of him, sis? I mean, other than the way he kisses."

"I'm going to hit you, cast or no cast."

He laughed.

"Not funny." she admonished, "I think Tyler Ashford has been through hell."

"True."

"But I don't know what we can do for him."

"I've been thinking about that. Maybe the only thing we can really do for him is just to be here. He's been a good friend to me."

"Yes. I think I like Mr. Ashford. I think I like him very much. But he and I are virtual strangers."

"It didn't look that way last night."

"Maxwell! I'm warning you!"

"How exactly did that happen, Ivory? I thought you always kept men at arm's length."

"I do. I don't know how it happened. Maybe it was the Masquerade Ball itself. Caught up in the moment, maybe a little too much to drink."

"That would explain acting a little foolish, maybe weaving when you walked, but that doesn't explain what I saw. That wasn't like you."

"So what?" she said irritably, "This is Venice. Aren't I entitled to act out of character now and then? I didn't know who he was then."

"Which is even stranger, if you ask me."

"Well, no one is asking you! What I do is my business. I don't question you on your many amorous adventures."

"But..."

"Enough! I refuse to discuss it any further."

At the knock on the door, Ivory jumped up and said, "I don't advise you to question Tyler like this."

"Don't worry. I wouldn't dream of it."

"You better behave yourself, Max."

"Yes, mam."

She opened the door, intending to invite Tyler in, but it wasn't Tyler. Two women stood before her. One was elderly, the other her own age. The younger one had straight blonde hair that fell past her shoulders to her waist. She was very pretty and wore a violet silk suit with a white blouse. She radiated class and her make up was expertly applied.

The older woman held her head high and wore a black suit with white cuffs and black gloves. A black pillbox hat adorned her silver hair that was in a neat bun. Her face was remarkable for her age. Only a few wrinkles at the corner of her eyes and mouth. She wore pink lipstick and was still very attractive with dark brows and large blue eyes. Ivory smiled slightly. "May I help you?"

The older woman spoke in a clear American accent, "You certainly can, my dear. My name is Victoria Ashford and this is my niece, Rochelle. We are looking for a Mr. Lawrence. I'm told this is his room."

Ivory stepped aside. "How do you do, Ms. Ashford? I'm Ivory Lawrence, Max's sister. Won't you please come in?"

"Pleased to meet you."

Rochelle nodded to Ivory as the two women stepped into the room. Ivory closed the door after them. Max looked surprised. Ivory said, "Please be seated."

Then she turned to Max. "This is Ms. Ashford and her niece, Rochelle."

Max grabbed his crutches. "Hello, there. Finally we meet."

He made his way over to the sitting area as the two

women settled on the sofa. Ivory couldn't help but notice Rochelle's eyes light up as she watched Max. "I received your message yesterday." he said.

"Yes. Well, we've just come from my sister's funeral. I persuaded my niece to come here before we went home. My brother Julian knows nothing about this."

She searched Max's face. "But you don't know who Julian is, do you?"

Max smiled at her. "On the contrary. Tyler told us about him."

The woman's face lit up. "You've spoken to Tyler?"

"Yes."

"Good Heavens. Then I was right in assuming Tyler was going to accompany you to the palazzo."

"Yes, you were. Tyler thought you would get his message through the telegram we sent."

"I was hoping, but I was also upset about my poor sister being killed and then you had your accident. Tell me, do you know what country my grandson is in now? I know he must move around a lot. But is there a way to get in touch with him? It would be most appreciated, Mr. Lawrence."

Ivory and Max exchanged glances. Max said, "Please call me Max."

"Very well. And I'm Victoria."

Max went on, "Victoria, your grandson is here."

"Here?" she said excitedly, "You mean here in Venice?"

"No, I mean here in this very inn."

She gasped. "Oh my Heavens! I just assumed he'd given up."

"No, no," Max assured her, "He left for a week or so but he returned yesterday. We were all trying to figure out how to get into the palazzo to see you."

"Oh my! This is such good news!"

Rochelle crossed her shapely legs and spoke for the first time, "Excuse me, Mr. Lawrence, but I'm a little confused. Aren't you the freelance writer who wanted to do an interview with my aunt?"

"Yes, I am."

"Then how do you know Tyler?"

"We're friends, Ms. Ashford. I do want an interview, but my main reason for becoming involved is Tyler himself. He asked for my help in getting into the palazzo."

"But why? He could've just come himself."

"He didn't know...listen, Tyler should be here to explain this himself. I'll call him right now."

Ivory handed him the phone and Rochelle said, "Don't tell him we're here. Let it be a surprise."

Max wasn't crazy about the idea but went along with it. Tyler wasn't in his room. "No answer," Max told them, "But I expect him at any moment."

Ivory said to Victoria, "You have been out of the public eye for many years. You were a great actress. I've always admired your talent."

Victoria smiled at her. "Thank you, my dear. That was so long ago. An eternity, it seems."

"If you don't mind my asking, why did you suddenly leave when your career was just beginning?"

Victoria looked at Max. "Are you sure you don't want your sister to do the interview? She seems very good at it."

Ivory was quick to say, "I hope I haven't offended you, Ms. Ashford."

"No, not at all. I was just teasing your brother."

Max grinned. "Now that you mention it, I had planned on sending Ivory in my place since I can't move around much."

"What a marvelous idea! That's what we'll do then. And in answer to your question, Miss Ivory, I left my career, fame, and fortune for love. I fell in love with the Earl of Eastwood, so I dropped everything and married him. Michael and I had ten years together, most of it right here in Venice.

He died of a heart attack and I decided to stay here after that, and eventually went back to my maiden name because of the family business. I don't usually get out much. I have everything I want at the palazzo. For years I didn't go out because of the press, or paparazzi, as it's referred to here.

They camped outside the palazzo at first. But I wanted to be left in peace to grieve for my dear Michael."

When a knock sounded on the door, everyone froze. Ivory went to open it. Tyler strode in while saying, "Sorry I'm late, but I took a walk to..."

He stopped when he saw the two women. Victoria stood up. Tyler went towards her hesitantly. "Grandmother? Is that you?"

She smiled, teary-eyed, and held out her arms as she said, "Of course it's me, my handsome grandson."

He hesitated a moment and then went to her and they embraced. Victoria said, "Oh, Tyler! It's so good to see you!"

She held him at arm's length. "Let me look at you. By God, you're a handsome man."

Rochelle was openly staring at her cousin, and she wasn't the only one. Ivory had only seen Tyler in his costume. He had been a Viking god then, and had been wearing make up to make his part more real. Now he was in jeans and a black shirt and she could only stare. His longish light blonde hair reached his shoulders and was brushed back from his face.

The light color of his hair stood out against the black shirt and his face was clean-shaven. He wasn't a Viking anymore, but somehow this was more startling. Last night she half believed she'd over-exaggerated his looks. But now in the light of day reality hit and she realized he was real. He was gorgeous and very real. Too real.

Her heart was beating erratically. This was absurd. She was at an age when this type of thing shouldn't be happening. She shouldn't be attracted to this man. She couldn't be. It was very important that she remain detached. She'd never had a problem with that before. It had always been easy.

She was just letting her imagination get the best of her. A few days in Venice and she was breaking all her own rules. Well, the Masquerade Ball was over and she had to get back to reality. Max was saying, "Why don't you three

44

go to Tyler's room? I'm sure you don't need us for your reunion."

Tyler turned to Ivory and for a moment he just looked at her. He'd walked right past her on his way in without looking at her. So that's what was underneath all that make up. He knew she'd be attractive but he hadn't been expecting to see such an exquisite beauty as this. He said, "I'd like you both to stay."

Ivory said quickly, "I'm afraid I can't. I have a lunch date."

Tyler frowned. "A lunch date? Now?"

"I'm afraid so."

Max asked, "Who are you having lunch with?"

"Antonio. We met last night. Please excuse me. It was nice meeting you, Ms. Ashford, Rochelle."

She turned and left the room quickly. Tyler turned to look pointedly at Max. When Max merely shrugged his shoulders, Tyler sat down. Victoria said, "We have so much to talk about, Grandson."

Tyler looked over at Rochelle. Victoria said, "This is your cousin, Rochelle."

Tyler smiled. "The last time I saw you, you were in pigtails and braces."

Rochelle smiled back. "And you were a skinny boy who was very quiet."

Tyler looked at Max. By unspoken mutual agreement, they knew now wasn't the time to discuss Rochelle's father."

Chapter Eight

Max went across the room with the aid of the crutches and sat on the bed. Rochelle rose as she said to her aunt, "Aunt Vicky, I'm rather hungry. Perhaps Mr. Lawrence could show me to the dining room where I could get something to eat."

She looked at Max and he stood back up. "Of course, but it will be slow going."

Victoria asked him, "Are you sure you don't mind?"

"No, not at all. My doctor told me to exercise more. I'm actually feeling better today."

They left and Tyler looked back at his grandmother. She leaned back on the sofa. Tyler didn't hesitate. "Why didn't you write to me all those years when I was in school? I wrote but you never answered."

Shock passed over her face. "What do you mean, Tyler? I wrote you several times. You are the one who never answered. Julian told me he called you and you were very angry with all of us and didn't want anything to do with the family. Then you left Europe and he said you traveled a lot but he could never find you."

Tyler clenched his jaw and his fists. "He lied. He never called me. It was Aunt Abby who finally wrote to me and told me it wouldn't be wise to return home. She sent me money and I went on my way. I never received your letters."

It was clear she was in a state of shock and confusion. "But I don't understand. My letters never returned."

"Well, I do understand. He kept them. Somehow he got a hold of your letters before they left the palazzo and when I wrote he kept those as well."

"I can't believe this! Why would he do such a thing?"

"It's time you opened your eyes concerning your brother. He's not the kind, caring man you think he is. He was cruel to me and he got rid of me because it was convenient for him to do so and he knew he could pull it off. I also think he was behind what happened to Maxwell."

"No, Tyler, that can't be."

"It can be and it is. He doesn't want me at the palazzo and he doesn't want Max there."

"But he didn't know you were coming."

"Maybe not, but he didn't want anyone interviewing you either."

"Well, that's true enough. He tried to discourage me from responding to Maxwell's inquiry and after I told him what had happened to Maxwell, he finally succeeded. He suggested that Maxwell was an unsavory character, and that we didn't need any more publicity, especially after what had happened to Abby."

Tyler paused. "What did happen to Aunt Abby, Grandmother?"

His grandmother replied with a shake of her head, "I don't really know. A maid found her in a part of the palazzo we don't use anymore. The police could find no clues of any kind."

"When I heard about it I was worried about you. That's why I wanted to come and see you. Something's going on there, Grandmother. Murder was committed, but who did it and why?"

"I don't know. Oh, I'm so confused. And I'll have to be going soon."

"Why? Uncle Julian doesn't know you're here, does he?"

She shook her head. "I don't know what to make of Julian lately. He's become so controlling. He seems worried and under a lot of pressure. He runs the family business and he runs our lives. I never minded before. I was content to let him run things. But he doesn't want me to leave the palazzo. When I want to go out for something, he always arranges for it to be brought to me.

He didn't want your friend to come. And if he kept our letters from getting to us he's even more controlling than I thought." She sighed and went on, "I just don't know what to make of all this. After Abby was murdered I began feeling frightened. I don't know who would murder her or what their reason could possibly be. But there's one thing that's perfectly clear to me, and in this I will have my way, no matter what my brother says or thinks."

"And what is that?"

"My grandson will be welcomed in my home and so will his friends."

She smiled at him. He grinned but then sobered. "We shouldn't have been kept apart, Grandmother. He had no right to do that."

"No, my dear boy, he did not. I want you to come with me, and bring that lovely girl, Ivory. We will have that interview and with you by my side, we will get to the bottom of this. The palazzo is mine and no one is going to make you feel unwelcome again. Will you come home with me, Tyler?"

He had to think about this for a few minutes. The palazzo was his home. It's where he should be. He'd planned on getting into the place, he just didn't know quite how. He had no idea what he would be walking into, and he didn't put anything past his uncle. Now his grandmother would be bringing him herself.

She had solved the problem for him by coming there. And they needed to spend time together. He wanted to make sure his grandmother wasn't being taken advantage of. His uncle was clever and crafty and no one knew that better than he. It was time to return to the palazzo. He wasn't a young boy anymore. He was a man and he needed to confront Julian.

There had to be a reason why he didn't want anyone there. And there had to be a reason why Aunt Abby was murdered. "I'll come with you, Grandmother. I'll talk to Ivory and Max. Will you wait here?"

She smiled. "Of course I will. I'm so delighted you're coming home."

"Yes, well I know someone who won't be."

Tyler found Max and Rochelle in the dining room. Off in a corner he saw Ivory and Antonio, as well. He went over to where Max was and spoke to his cousin, "Rochelle, Grandmother is waiting for you. I need to talk to Max."

She smiled at both men. "Of course. I was finished and getting ready to go anyway."

She stood up and after saying goodbye to Max, she left. Tyler sat down. "We need to talk."

"Right. I'll go get Ivory."

"That's okay, I'll do it. It will be my pleasure."

He went directly over to Ivory's table and looked only at her when he said, "Ivory, your brother and I need to talk to you. It's very important."

Then he walked back to Max and sat down. Antonio tossed down his napkin. "Well, that was kind of rude."

"He just has other things on his mind. You'll have to excuse me, Antonio."

"But when can I see you again?"

"I don't really know. As I told you, I'm only here for a short visit. Thank you for lunch."

"But you sound so final. Like we'll never see each other again or spend time together."

"I'm sorry, but that may very well be the case. Goodbye, Antonio."

She left the table quickly and joined Tyler and her brother. Max grinned at her. "Your date seems a little upset."

"He'll get over it. Now what's going on?"

She was sitting next to Tyler since the space on the seat next to Max was occupied with his crutches. The seat wasn't very wide so she and Tyler were elbow to elbow. He put his arm on the back of the seat behind her and leaned back as he said, "A lot is going on. My grandmother has asked me to go home with her and she mentioned you, Ivory, coming with us. For the interview. But we don't have a lot of time to decide this. My uncle doesn't know she's here. I've told her what I think about him and she now has serious doubts.

49

She did tell me that she wrote me while I was in school. He kept our letters from getting to one another.

It's time for me to confront him. There's also my aunt's murder to think about. And why Julian doesn't want anyone at the palazzo. You both knew I wanted to find out what's been going on there. And now it's time for you to make a decision. If you want to go home and let me handle this, I won't hold it against you. However, I could use all the help and support I can get. It's up to you."

Max and Ivory exchanged glances. Max said, "I'm going to stay here for awhile. Until I'm feeling better. Ivory, if you want to go home I'll try to do the interview on my own later on."

She looked from her brother to Tyler and then back to her brother again. "I'm not leaving you here, Max. I said I wanted to help and I haven't changed my mind."

She turned to Tyler. "When do we leave?"

He grinned at them both. "As soon as you're packed."

Ivory had deep reservations about leaving her brother. She didn't want to leave him at all, but she was determined to come back and check on him real soon. None of them had any idea how long this whole thing would take. Of course, she was free to leave whenever she wanted. She'd do the interview and then would see how things stood.

She was curious about Tyler's family. Besides, she had no job to get back to and she fully intended on seeing all there was to see in Venice before she left. No sense in wasting this trip. So Ivory decided to look upon it as a long deserved holiday.

They loaded up their suitcases on a gondola and Rochelle and Victoria rode in a separate one. It was the only arrangements they could make on such short notice. Ivory looked around at the water and sights as they went smoothly along. Tyler was quiet beside her. After a few minutes she looked over at him. He smiled at her. "Thank you for doing this, Ivory."

"That's okay. I can think of worse things other than seeing Venice and spending time at a palazzo."

He was thoughtful again. Ivory could tell he had a lot on his mind. She supposed they all did. She'd said goodbye to her brother and it had been very hard to leave him. It had always been that way whenever they parted.

Tyler spoke, startling her out of her musings, "Max and I were talking earlier, while you were getting your things together and ...well...we think it would be a good idea if you went to the palazzo as my wife."

Ivory just stared at him and was quite speechless. "What?"

"Just hear me out. If you go as my wife it will be much safer for you. My uncle doesn't want outsiders there, and if he arranged what happened to Max, it would be dangerous for you to conduct this interview. As my wife you could have your interview and my uncle need never know. I'm not sure what we'll be walking into, Ivory, but I'd feel better if everyone thought you were my wife. My grandmother agrees, incidentally."

Ivory found her voice quickly. "Well, I'm so glad everyone agrees!"

"Now, Ivory, this is no time to be difficult."

"Difficult! Is that what you think I'm being? I think I'm the only one who's thinking rationally here. Married people know each other well. We've only known each other a couple of days. It will never work."

"So we'll be newlyweds and we'll have to act like we're man and wife. It's worth it to ensure your safety. It's also important for my uncle to know you're off limits."

"I see. Now you don't think I can handle your uncle. I've been handling men for years, Tyler Ashford."

"He's different."

"I resent you and Max thinking I can't take care of myself. Besides, your uncle is married."

"Not anymore. His wife left him several years ago for another man. They're divorced."

"So what?"

"So I want you to go along with me on this. You said you wanted to help. This is the way I want you to help. It isn't about whether or not you can handle men or not. I want to protect you. As my wife you wouldn't be an outsider and my uncle would be less likely to think of you as a threat."

Ivory thought seriously about what he was saying. He had some good points but she was trying to keep him at a distance. How on earth could she do that when everyone would think she was his wife? But on the other hand, she would feel a little safer going as his wife. She also wouldn't feel so awkward. But it was too bizarre.

Tyler watched her closely. "Ivory, I've done some thinking about this. It will work."

She looked at him. "Married people share the same room, occupy the same bed."

He grinned.

"Tyler!"

"Okay, okay. I've worked that one out, as well. We can occupy my parents' old quarters. They're in a completely different section of the palazzo. The east wing. There are two bedrooms off of a living room. Like an apartment. We'd have privacy and no one would be the wiser."

That made her feel a little better, at least. Being with him constantly in a bedroom would drive her crazy. She said, "I don't think this is a good idea."

"But you'll consider it?"

"Yes, I'll consider if for all the twenty minutes or so that it takes us to get to the palazzo. You could've mentioned this sooner, you know."

"I just thought of it about an hour ago."

"And Max agreed?"

"He did. In fact, it eased his mind somewhat. He's worried about you."

"I'm worried about me too."

"Well, don't. I won't let anything happen to you."

Ivory wasn't used to hearing those words. Actually, it was kind of nice. She'd always taken care of herself. And now this very capable man was telling her he would protect her. This was crazy. What was she getting herself into? It was all becoming so complicated. Now she had to be an actress, as well. She could refuse to go along with this.

It would probably be the best thing for her nerves, but not the wisest decision considering the situation. Imagine. Being Tyler Ashfords wife. The thought unnerved her more than a little. But it was just a part she would be playing. Nothing more. And when she decided to leave he could always tell his family they had a fight and split up. Could this actually work?

Maybe his family would feel more comfortable around his wife than an outsider. Ivory couldn't believe she was actually considering this crazy plan. Well, why not? This could be something she would always remember. Her adventure in Venice. She looked over at him. He was looking out at the view. She smiled.

Such a good-looking husband he would be. She broke the silence. "Well? What kind of husband are you? I don't even have a wedding ring!"

He turned to her with disbelief written over his face. He never thought she'd go along with it. "You'll do it?"

"I'll do it, but I don't think it's the wisest decision I've ever made."

"It's our only solution."

"Is it?"

"You know it is."

"Well, you did make some very good points, but I've never done anything like this before."

"I know," he assured her, "Neither have I."

He reached in his pocket and pulled out some tissue. She took it from him, opened it, and then gasped when she saw the diamond and emerald ring. She looked up at him in astonishment. He said, "My grandmother gave that to me so you could wear it as a wedding ring. It was my mother's at one time."

She could tell by his attitude that this was a sore subject so she didn't say anything. He shook off his memories, took the ring from her, and slipped it on her finger. "Consider yourself married."

She looked at his hand and saw that he was wearing a gold ring with an emerald. It sort of matched the ring she was wearing. He saw where she was looking so he said, "This was my father's ring. I keep it with me at all times. It seems appropriate for what we have in mind."

"It's very beautiful."

They were quiet then. Ivory could tell that thinking about his parents and the past had upset him. We all had our bad moments, she supposed. After a few minutes they began slowing down. Ivory looked about her. There were several tall buildings, all palazzo's. The gondola was turning towards one certain dock and she looked up at the four story Venetian building.

Tyler said as he sat forward, "This is it. Palazzo Delegado. Would you care to know something about it?"

"Yes, please. It's so beautiful and gothic."

"There are centuries of scandals and murder at this palazzo. There are only two ways to get in and out of it; at the dock here and also through the walled garden. It's gothic, as you said. If you look at it you can see that it has round Renaissance arches and pilasters from the Byzantine era. My grandmother's family bought it in 1930. It had been sitting empty for a few years. It originally belonged to Giovanni Daridos.

He was a Chancery secretary who negotiated peace with the Turks in 1479. He was very successful in Constantinople, so he built this Renaissance palazzo. He added the inscription: 'To the spirit of the city'. They say it is cursed. It all began when Daridos's daughter died of a broken heart after she married into a patrician family. A Barbaro family. The Barbaro dynasty retained this palazzo until the 19th century and scandals and disasters have always surrounded it. Most of the family was massacred."

"My God. That is a disaster."

"Quite. The local Venetians were afraid to buy it, but an American merchant finally did. And then he went bankrupt and died penniless. Then there was Robert Brown in the

54

1840's. He was an Englishman who committed suicide in the drawing room. You still want me to go on?"

"Yes, of course."

"Sixty years after that, in 1900, a melancholic French poet named Henri de Reginor moved in but died shortly after. Natural causes, as far as I know. After Henri came Charles Burke, and what a guy he was. He was American and it was reported that he held orgies of all kinds in the palazzo and was finally expelled from the city. In 1905, Lucien Lamberto, a well-known pianist, was murdered and the case was never solved. A count named Giodanaia Lonzo bought it in 1910 and his mistress battered him to death. She did it with a candlestick."

"Please tell me this gets better."

"Afraid not. A Venetian finally bought it in 1915 and the maid murdered the owners. Since then it remained empty until my great-grandfather bought it."

"And what happened to him?"

"Nothing. He died of natural causes."

"Amazing. So your family broke the curse."

"Well, until my aunt died."

"But that surely has nothing to do with the curse. Nothing had happened in over sixty years."

"Yes, but you have to remember that the palazzo stood empty for all those years. Still, I'm not superstitious. See the enclosed terraces on each floor? It is Arabian in design. Inside are high ceilings, chandeliers of Murano glass, and carved columns of Istrian stone. The palazzo is so big it has four wings, all attached and in the center is a garden-like courtyard with a Venetian fountain and greenery as well as colorful flowers. My parents' rooms are up there to the left. And from there you can see a lot of Venice."

"I noticed that the neighboring buildings are sort of close to one another, but the palazzo is separated by a high brick wall covered in ivy or some kind of shrubbery."

"Yes. I'm not sure if the residents of the palazzo were trying to maintain privacy or the neighbors built the walls so they wouldn't be able to see the palazzo and therefore not be jinxed."

The gondola stopped and the gondolier got out and tied it to a green and white striped pole at the dock. Tyler stood up as he asked her, "Are you afraid to go in, now that I've told you about its horrid history?"

She took his hand and he helped her onto the stone dock." Not at all. Its history just makes it more fascinating."

The palazzo was white with pale yellow trim. There was an oval stone archway in front of them that led up to the entrance of the place. Each floor had four mosaic-style windows next to each other on the left sides and a single window on the right. And that was just this side of it. Now Ivory could see just how large the palazzo was. It was gothic, beautiful, and bewitching. God, she loved challenges.

Chapter Nine

The inside of the palazzo was even more amazing than the outside. As Ivory looked around her at all the artwork, elaborate furniture, antiques and chandeliers, it was hard to believe that so many devastating things had happened there in the past. It really was a palace. The architecture was old and there were many windows with velvet draperies adorning them. On the floors were Persian, Oriental, French, and American style rugs. It was too much to take in all at once.

The minute they'd come inside, Rochelle had made a hasty retreat. A housekeeper and maid had met them and a male servant took their luggage. There was no one else present and Ivory was glad. She wasn't up to meeting anyone just yet. She couldn't believe how many different rooms there were. Rooms of all sizes. Victoria retired to her quarters after Tyler assured her they'd be fine.

He led Ivory down a long hallway that circled onto a wide ascending carpeted staircase. He said, "This part of the palazzo wasn't used after my mother left. The rooms that are used are at the front of the palazzo. At least that's the way it used to be. It doesn't look like much has changed. It's almost as if I only left yesterday."

"This must be difficult for you. You've been gone a long time."

"Yes, I have. I never thought I would step foot in this place again."

At the top of the stairs they rounded a corner and were in another hallway that ran both ways. Doors were positioned here and there, some distance away from each other. They turned left and towards the end of the corridor, was a huge oak door. There were no more doors after this one and at the very end of the hallway was a tall window where light poured through it onto the Turkish carpet.

Tyler opened the door and let Ivory go in first. She

caught her breath. She was standing in a very large living room that looked like it belonged in the 19th century. Directly across the wide expanse of the room were the four windows she'd seen from outside. In the center of the room were two Victorian settees with Queen Anne chairs on each side. They circled a glass coffee table that was held up by a ceramic statue of a white elephant.

As she circled the room she said, "Oh, Tyler, this is beautiful. And so huge. I feel like I'm in another century."

He didn't reply. He was looking around himself. Probably reliving painful memories, Ivory thought. Just inside the door, in the left corner was a mahogany roll-top desk with matching chair. A floor-length lamp with a red pleated shade stood beside it.

To the right of the room were floor to ceiling bookshelves. There were four of them altogether and they were filled with books of different sizes and categories. In front of the bookshelves were a couple of red velvet high-back chairs with a small dark glass table positioned between them. On the table was a reading lamp of brass with a dark green pleated shade. Beyond the bookshelves was another huge oak door. One of the bedrooms, no doubt.

Beyond the door in the right corner was a white marble fireplace. The windows were on the other side of this. Two more red velvet chairs were positioned in front of the fireplace. On the mantle was an assortment of miniature figurines that ranged from wild animals to Victorian ladies. On the other side of the room was another mahogany table with a bust of a Victorian maiden. On the left side of the windows was a door with glass panes.

This obviously opened onto the enclosed balcony she'd seen from below. Ivory could only stare at it all. Tyler opened the door to the left and they went into a large bedroom. The center of the room was taken up with a large four poster bed made of mahogany. Above the bed, attached to the ceiling, was a large brass ring and from this streamed a white gauze curtain that flowed over the high bedposts and fell to the floor.

The bedspread was dark green satin. Positioned about the room was the various furniture; an antique dresser, vanity table, and two chairs that stood in front of another fireplace to the left of the bed. And to the left of the fireplace was a glass panel door where Ivory could see another balcony. She turned to Tyler but he'd already left the room. She went back into the main salon and saw that the other bedroom door was open.

She went over to it. This room was done in dark brown and beige. There was another four poster bed, but this one had no canopy netting. A rich brown velvet spread covered the bed. The set up was the same with the fireplace and balcony door. This had obviously been a man's bedroom. Tyler said as he sat down on the bed, "At one time this was my nursery and bedroom."

"These are lovely rooms, Tyler. You were lucky to live here as a child."

"I guess you're right. Over the years unhappiness seemed to blind me to all this."

Ivory didn't know if she should try and comfort him. He wouldn't appreciate her pity. Sensing that he needed some time alone, she said, "I'm a little tired, Tyler. If it's okay with you, I'll take the other room. I think I could use a nap."

"Yes, you take that room. That was my parents' room." The melancholy pervaded the very air.

"Thank you," she said and left.

When she went back into the main room she saw their luggage inside the door. Picking up her suitcases, she went to her new room. She set the cases down and went to open the door to the balcony that ran the length of the room. The canal of Venice was below her. She breathed deeply and then went in to take her nap.

Ivory hadn't had a problem drifting right off to sleep in strange surroundings. Oddly enough, she'd felt right at home in her new quarters and slept deeply. In fact, she slept for over an hour. When she woke she sat up and looked around her. Where was the bathroom? There was a door to the right of the room and also one directly across from the bed. She went to that one first and found that it was a rather large closet and there were clothes hanging there.

A switch hanging from the light revealed that the clothes were mostly gowns and there was a huge floor-length mirror towards the back of the closet. No other types of clothes were visible and there were no shoes on the floor. Just a dozen or so gowns hanging to the left. The other door was the bathroom. Light poured from a single window.

In front of the window was a square tub the size of a Jacuzzi, and there were no curtains adorning the window, so one could take a bath and have a view at the same time. The view consisted of the tall hedge she'd seen earlier and the canal as well as parts of Venice. Everything else about the room was ordinary but the tub was magnificent.

Dark blue tiles encircled it with brass fixtures. Ivory turned on the water. This was too inviting and she planned on indulging herself. Once emerged in hot water, she leaned back against the curved part of the tub and closed her eyes. She could deal with not having a shower. Opening her eyes, she looked down at part of Venice, the canal itself. Darkness was descending. The day was fading away, and Ivory knew she'd never felt more relaxed and content than she did at that moment.

No matter if Julian Ashford didn't like her or want her there. She had this tub. No matter if things didn't go well and Tyler and his uncle yelled at each other and made everyone miserable. She had this tub. No matter if she had a horrible time while she was there, the food was terrible and posing as Tyler's wife was disastrous and she felt as though she couldn't stand it another minute. She had this tub. She could always run in there and lock herself in.

Tyler was sitting on one of the chairs in front of the bookshelves. A crystal goblet was in his hand, and when he saw Ivory he just looked at her for a minute. She was wearing black slacks and a white sweater. He said, "I was beginning to wonder if I was going to have to wake you."

She nodded to his drink and asked, "Where'd you get

that?"

He reached over to the glass table beside his chair and pulled out a long cart with assorted decanters and a couple of glasses on it. The cart rolled to and fro easily but you couldn't actually see it was there because the front of the table looked like the cart was merely a drawer. An oval brass handle pulled the cart out. She smiled. "Very clever. I could use a drink. White wine would be nice."

As he poured her wine she sat on the other chair near him. He asked her, "How'd you sleep?"

"Wonderfully. And that spectacular tub and I have formed a lasting relationship."

He laughed. "My mother had that tub imported from Rome."

"Clever woman. I especially liked the angels painted on the bottom."

"Yes, she was clever enough to leave Venice. I don't imagine she and my uncle got along too well."

"Do you remember that?"

"A little. My mother was very headstrong. She didn't like people telling her what to do. I know she felt stifled here. My father was the opposite. He loved it here. The place fascinated him. That's how I know all about the history of this place. My father told me."

"How nice. I envy you, Tyler Ashford."

"Well, I envy you."

"Me? Why?"

He handed her the glass of wine. "Because you and Maxwell have always had each other. I had no one I could turn to."

"You had your grandmother."

"For awhile. But now I have her back so let's not dwell on the past."

"That could be difficult."

"Not really. You're here with me now and your presence changes things. This is all new to you. I'm seeing it again through your eyes. I will deal with the past. I've thought of little else for the past couple of hours. But the

61

fact is I'm no longer a young boy living here with dark shadows hanging over me. Things are different for me now. Your presence helps tremendously."

"Glad to be of service. Now, when's dinner?"

"At seven. That's about thirty minutes from now. Perhaps you should go and change for dinner."

The glass stopped halfway to her mouth. "Change?"

"Yes, for dinner."

She was momentarily speechless. She had to dress formally for dinner. Tyler said, "It's a tradition here. That's part of the past the palazzo will always hold onto."

"You're talking about gowns."

He laughed. "Yes, exactly."

"I don't have any formal gowns with me. I didn't realize I would be dining with Venetian society."

"There should be some in your closet. The palazzo always keeps extra gowns in the closets for guests. My mother probably left some also."

"Well, I did see some gowns in the closet. What if they aren't my size?"

"Come on. Let's go have a look."

He followed her to the closet. Once inside she went to pull the chain for the light and when she turned back around she ran into Tyler. His arms went around her to steady her. She looked up into his blue eyes. "Sorry."

He looked down at her and instead of releasing her, he kept his hands on her waist. Her gaze went over his white cotton dress shirt that was open at the collar. His hair was neatly combed back and he was clean-shaven. The look he gave her was searching.

She bit her bottom lip and said softly, "You can let go of me now."

As his head lowered she began to panic and backed away, nearly falling into the mirror in the process. He reached out a hand to steady her. "Careful."

"I'm fine. Can we look at the clothes now?"

"Are you sure that's what you'd rather be doing?"

His sensual deep voice penetrated her and she almost

gave in. Instead, she pulled herself together and replied, "Of course I'm sure. We have to go down to dinner."

He looked at her a moment longer and then turned to the clothes. He ran a hand through them, inspecting a few.

"These look like they'd fit you. Pick one you like."

"Ty, I think it would be best if we concentrate on our reason for being here. I'm only here playing a part. The part of being your wife. It would be best if we were emotionally detached."

"Probably." he answered.

"Then you agree?" she asked, "You agree we should try to keep a little distance between us?"

"I didn't say that."

"Come on, Tyler. You must see that any emotional involvement would be a mistake."

"You really put your cards right out on the table, don't you?"

He turned to leave. She went after him. "Will you at least promise me you won't try to kiss me again?"

"No."

And then he left the room, closing the door after him. Ivory didn't know whether she was pleased or upset by his answer.

Chapter Ten

When Ivory came out of her room the second time she looked quite different. She wore a gown of pale yellow silk. It was simple in design; long fitted sleeves and a round neckline. It was gathered at the waist and she'd put her hair up in a French roll. She wore deep red lipstick and brown eye shadow. The Masquerade Ball was over but Tyler thought she still looked like a queen. She wore her own white heels and no jewelry other than amethyst teardrop earrings.

He couldn't help but notice her full breasts above the neckline. Did she have to look so damn sexy and elegant at the same time? She was exquisite. Unfortunately, his uncle would think so as well. But he was past caring. She was a vision and would be quite impressive. "You look great, Ivory. That color goes good with your black hair."

She smiled at him. He went to take her arm and they left the room. Tyler was wearing a black suit now and he looked very handsome. They went back down the stairs and continued down a wide hall until they came upon the dining room. Everyone was already there when they entered. Ivory knew that the distinguished silver-haired man at the end of the table was Julian Ashford.

At the opposite end was Victoria and on one side of the rather long table were Rochelle and a young man. Victoria smiled at them and said, "Tyler, we were just talking about you."

"I can well imagine." he said as he led Ivory to a seat across from Rochelle, and he took the seat next to her, making it so he was the closest to his uncle. Julian looked at his nephew first with a narrowed expression, and then he looked at Ivory and his expression changed. He looked back at Tyler. "Hello, Tyler. Welcome home."

'He actually acts as though he means it.' Tyler thought.

"Thanks, Uncle."

Julian looked back at Ivory and smiled. "And who is this exquisite lady?"

Tyler stiffened and then replied, "This is Ivory, my wife. Ivory, this is my uncle, Julian."

Julian seemed surprised. Obviously Victoria hadn't told him about Ivory. Julian smiled at her. "Nice to meet you, Ivory. What a lovely name you have. It fits you so well."

"Thank you."

Tyler spoke to her, "You haven't met Julian's son, Austin, yet. Austin, this is Ivory. Ivory, my cousin Austin."

Austin smiled at her. "It's a pleasure to meet you, Ivory."

She smiled and inclined her head. Austin was about thirty years of age. He was a handsome man with brown eyes and light brown hair that reached his collarbone. He had what was referred to as aristocratic features. Almost too handsome. He wore a brown suit with a tan shirt and black tie. Julian was attractive as well. He had a gray mustache and closely trimmed beard.

He reminded Ivory of Sean Connery in a way. He wore a navy blue suit with a white shirt and red tie, was very fit and trim and didn't look much over sixty. When he smiled at her his dimples appeared and she could tell he used that smile of his to its fullest advantage. The meal went smoothly as Tyler's family asked him how he'd been, where he'd been, and his line of work. Rochelle asked most of the questions, but so did Austin and Victoria.

Tyler told them he had several enterprises. He owned a shopping mall in Texas, a bottled water plant in Switzerland, and a five-story exclusive hotel in New York. Julian was listening to everyone else. When he did speak, it was to Ivory, "Tell me, my dear, where did you meet my nephew?"

She looked over at him. Tyler held his breath. They hadn't discussed this. She replied easily, "At a Masquerade Ball here in Venice."

She dearly wished she could see Tyler's face at that moment, but she kept her gaze on his uncle. Julian raised and eyebrow. "Indeed? How unusual."

"Yes, it was actually. He was Thor, the Viking God, and I was Cleopatra."

Julian looked at Tyler. "You've been living here then?"

Tyler shook his head. "No. I've only been here a short while."

Victoria said, "The two of you are still newlyweds. How wonderful."

Austin asked Ivory where she was from and she told him. She had just come to Venice on a holiday. Austin asked her what her occupation had been and she told him she'd been a secretary. Julian didn't ask Tyler another direct question and Tyler didn't address his uncle either. Ivory rather liked Austin. He was a witty, humorous, intelligent man. The two of them kept the conversation going. Ivory was aware that Julian watched her and Tyler.

He seemed like a nice enough man on the surface. Hardly capable of the things Tyler had accused him of. And that meant he was clever. Very clever indeed. If she hadn't known better, if Tyler had never told her about him, she would probably have liked Julian very much. But now she was troubled. Julian was too smart to let anything slip. If something were going on there he would be careful not to let anyone know what it was.

Julian excused himself immediately after dinner. He told Ivory it had been nice to meet her and didn't address or even look at anyone else before leaving the room. After he left, Victoria stood up. "I must retire as well, I'm afraid. Tyler, we must have a visit tomorrow."

She looked at Ivory. "Would you care to have lunch tomorrow, my dear?"

Ivory smiled and said she would like that. Tyler and Ivory walked her out as they said their goodnights to Austin and Rochelle. Once back in their rooms, Ivory asked, "Well? How do you think it went?"

Tyler sat on the sofa. "As well as could be expected, I guess. You don't know how difficult it was not to confront him then and there. He was so superior and smug. What did you think of him?"

She sat across from him. "He seemed charming and very distinguished."

"Well, don't let that fool you. He's a crafty snake in sheep's clothing. But I think it was a good beginning. He seemed to be taken with you. I knew he would."

They looked at each other. Tyler said, "It's been a long day."

"Are you tired?"

"A little, yes. I didn't sleep very well last night."

"Well then, we should say goodnight."

There was an awkward silence, so without further delay Ivory got up and went to her room. Tyler hadn't spoken again. She thought he was in an odd mood, but completely understandable considering all that was happening. She went out onto the balcony to look down at the canal. People were traveling in gondolas.

The palazzo was lit up on the outside with a few lights and the light glistened on the water and seemed to have a hypnotic effect. Some time much later, she went back in to go to bed.

Tyler sat where he was for awhile. There hadn't been anything to say to Ivory. He didn't know what was going to happen now. No one in the palazzo, the members of his family, seemed to be capable of murder. And as much as he resented his uncle, he couldn't see him strangling his own sister. Maybe the palazzo curse had returned after over sixty years of silence. Just waiting for a family to move in. If that was the case, then it had certainly waited long enough.

But that was absurd. He didn't believe in curses. Especially curses on buildings. There had to be another explanation. The previous occupants had brought their bad luck upon themselves. Abby had been murdered for a reason. A very specific reason and he had to find out what that reason was. Jesus, he was worn out. He took his troubled thoughts and went to his room with them.

Ivory was refreshed the next morning and decided to

explore the palazzo. It was such a huge place and she needed to familiarize herself with it if she was to get around on her own. From what she'd seen so far, the main rooms surrounded the garden area. It was early. Barely eight o'clock. If Tyler wasn't up yet she'd let him sleep. No need to disturb him. Dressing casually in jeans and a pale green pullover sweater, she put her hair up once again.

She'd been too tired the night before to light a fire and the room was chilly. She slid a note-pad and pen in her sweater's pocket for the interview. They'd probably conduct it over lunch. Max had filled her in on what he needed; all information about Victoria's past and the Ashford family members. Max intended on writing a novel of fiction using information Victoria supplied.

Her privacy would be kept intact. No one would know it was the Ashfords he was writing about. He probably wouldn't use all of what she said, but it was a work of fiction and up to the author. Of course the interview wasn't the true reason for coming to the palazzo. It was just an excuse. But Max intended to take advantage of the situation anyway.

He was a good writer. He'd written five novels already, and for three of them he's used this method. Nobody ever knew his work was based on real people. He'd interviewed a veteran who'd lost both legs in the Vietnam War, a millionaire who'd come from an orphanage, and a female rock star who'd come from drugs and violence on skid-row to get her life together and become a respected and well known singer.

He did it all with the help of real people and no one ever guessed it was all based on the truth. When she went out into the other room, Tyler was no where in sight. She remembered the way to the dining room. It was between the library and the kitchen, the library being towards the front of the house, and opening onto the garden. The minute she walked into the dining room a maid came out of the kitchen and asked her what she wanted to eat.

No one else was there. The maid, who introduced herself as Danielle, told her Victoria usually had breakfast on

68

her balcony, Mr. Julian hardly ever showed up for breakfast, but Miss Rochelle and Mr. Austin met here in the dining room like clockwork at nine o'clock every morning. After she brought her coffee, Ivory sat back and looked out the glass doors at the garden beyond. All she could see was a shrubbery wall with roses threading through it.

A patio of white stones surrounded the garden area. The shrubbery and rose bushes enclosed the main part of the garden so she couldn't see beyond from where she sat. Ivory found it all very interesting. She'd never been in a house that had a garden indoors. Ah, life in Venice. How different her life could've been if she'd grown up in a place like this. But perhaps she wouldn't have appreciated it as much as she did now. Did the Ashfords take it all for granted? Did Tyler?

Chapter Eleven

Victoria sat on the balcony at a small glass table. She was still in her violet silk robe and white satin slippers. Her silver hair was pulled back from her face with a black ribbon. She'd already had her breakfast and was now having her coffee as she waited for her brother. She had summoned him earlier. She had no intention of ignoring what she suspected about him. Victoria intended to confront her brother and find out the truth.

"You asked to see me?"

Julian, in brown slacks and a tan shirt, approached the table and sat down across from her. "Coffee?" she asked.

He nodded and she poured him a cup. As she slid the cup and saucer over to him he asked impatiently, "What is it, Vicky? I'm really busy. I need to get back to my office."

"You can take a few minutes to talk to me. We hardly see each other. We get together at dinner and that's it."

"Surely you exaggerate."

"Not really, Julian."

He sighed, drank some coffee, and asked, "Well? What did you want to talk to me about?"

"I think you know, Julian. It's about Tyler."

He said nothing, just watched her. She raised an articulate eyebrow. "Well? No comment?"

"I'm waiting for you to continue. What about Tyler?"

"I want to know why you kept my letters from getting to him and why you kept his letters from me."

"I see you aren't asking, but telling me I did this."

"That's right."

"Very well, I won't deny it. I did keep his letters from you. I didn't think it was a good idea to give them to you. I didn't want you to be upset."

Victoria demanded angrily, "What right do you have to decide anything concerning Tyler and I? It's none of your damn business!"

Julian looked taken back. His sister had never raised her voice to him. At least, not in a very long time. But she wasn't finished with him yet.

"This is my house, Julian! You live here at my request. You run the family business because I allow you to. The business was passed down to my husband and then to me. I've let you take over because I was never interested in it. But damn it, Julian, not everything in this house is yours to take over! You don't rule me.

I make my own decisions. This is my grandson we're talking about. You have done us both a great injustice. He thought I'd abandoned him all these years and I thought he didn't want anything to do with us. And I thought that because you told me so. You lied about talking to him on the phone. That never happened at all."

"I was under the impression that he wanted to go his own way and that he didn't want our help."

"And how did you come to that conclusion?"

"What is this, Vicky? Why all the questions now? You've never asked me about it before."

"And that's because I never dreamed you could be so cruel!"

"Cruel! I was looking out for you. It's nice to see how much all my efforts have been appreciated."

"Oh, knock it off. Don't go there, Julian. You weren't looking out for me. For some reason you didn't want Tyler here. And I would really like to know what that reason was."

"Don't you know?" he shot back, "Can't you guess? Tyler was showing signs of being a troublemaker and a spoiled brat. I didn't want any of his bad habits rubbing off on Rochelle and Austin."

"But he had every right to be here! He had more of a right than your children did. He's my son's son. And you had no right to lie to me in an effort to get rid of him. You said his father told you in confidence that he wanted Tyler to go to school away from Venice. But I don't think he told you any such thing. Tyler is my heir. This place will go to him some day, and so will the business."

Julian's eyes narrowed. He was trying to keep his temper in check, she could tell. He said, "I thought you changed your will. I had no idea Tyler was still your heir."

"What made you think that?"

"You saw your attorney about a year after Tyler left. I assumed you were changing your will."

"I was not changing it, I was merely adding to it. I've made provisions for you and your children."

"May I ask what they are?"

She hesitated. "I didn't want to get into this right now, but you may as well know. Tyler is my heir. Everything will go to him except for the following things; twenty-five percent of the business goes to you and ten percent to your children, at five percent each. They will also receive fifty thousand dollars each and you a hundred and fifty, upon my death."

"I don't understand. The Ashford Company is only worth a couple million, and most of it is tied up. How can you dole out that kind of money without first selling the business?"

She smiled at him indulgently. "It's true that most of our assets are tied up in the company, but the family business isn't the whole source of my wealth. Granted, the property business has always been lucrative, but Father left me with much more than that."

"What are you talking about?"

"The Ashford jewels."

"The Ashford jewels! That can't be. They've been missing since Father died. We looked for them and couldn't find them."

"I know where they are. Abby found them. They're here in the palazzo. He hid them, you see, and we left them where they are. They couldn't be safer. When I die there are instructions in my will to sell them. Then two hundred and fifty five thousand goes to you, Rochelle, and Austin, and the remaining balance goes to Tyler."

"But they must be worth several million dollars by

now."

"They are."

"Do you mind my asking why you're giving Tyler so much money?"

"I don't mind, Julian. Michael worried about our son and his family. He wanted them always to be taken care of. Daddy gave the jewels to me. You heard that in his will. They were his mothers. You know the story. Anyway, Michael and I never questioned where they were until Daddy's death. We just assumed, as I'm sure you did that he had them in some vault or something. In his will he left them to me but didn't tell anyone where they were.

We all forgot about it after awhile but Michael and I made a deal. If they were ever found they would go to our son. After his death, I stipulated in my will that they would then go to Tyler. However, I decided to give you and your children a portion of it. I never thought we'd find them. But Abby never forgot them. She must've been searching for them all along. But a deal is a deal. And I intend to keep that promise. I would've given Abby a portion also but that's no longer possible."

"When did she find them?"

"About six months ago. I'd never seen her so excited. She said she had clues. I never really paid much attention to her ramblings. I put it in my will but I never actually believed we'd ever find them."

Julian's head was spinning. "Why didn't you tell me all this before?"

"Abby didn't want anyone to know."

"So what? My God, you listened to her? I'm your brother. He was my father too."

Victoria didn't reply. He knew what she was thinking. Long ago, he'd been disowned by their father. Julian hadn't even been mentioned in the will. It was Victoria who had welcomed him into her home after Vincent Ashford had died.

"I'm sorry, Julian." Victoria spoke softly, "Perhaps I should have told you. But Abby and I didn't want anyone knowing. It seemed better to keep it to ourselves and leave them where they are. Abby made me swear that I'd never tell anyone where they were."

"And are you going to keep that promise?"

"Of course I will."

"Damn it, Vicky! I have a right to know!"

"I'm sorry, Julian, but you really don't. They are my inheritance."

Julian was very upset. He stood up. Victoria said, "We haven't finished talking about what you did to Tyler."

"What's done is done. Talking about it isn't going to change it. Besides, it looks as if Tyler will be well compensated for anything I've done."

He walked away then and Victoria decided to let the matter drop. The revelation of the jewels had been quite a shock to him. Perhaps she shouldn't have told him. She'd broken her promise to Abby. Her sister hadn't wanted Julian to know about the jewels and she hadn't wanted him to know where they were located.

Well, he now knew about them but he didn't know where they were. So she'd kept half of the promise. Julian would get over it. Besides, he'd be receiving a lot of money one-day. Victoria thought she was being more than generous.

Chapter Twelve

When Tyler finally got up it was to discover that Ivory had already left. So he went to his grandmother's room. She was now fully dressed and on the terrace having her last cup of coffee. She brightened when she saw him.

"Thank God it's you."

He sat in the same chair his uncle had occupied earlier.

"Who did you think it was?"

"Julian."

"He was here?"

"Yes, I confronted him about keeping our letters from each other."

Tyler frowned. "Did he deny it?"

"No. He said he did it for me. I let him know what I thought, of course. And then we got into something else."

"What?"

"Your inheritance. I told him you were my heir and that the bulk of my estate would go to you."

One of Tyler's eyebrows rose and he seemed very surprised. And then she told him about the Ashford jewels. Of course he remembered them. His father, Jason, had told him about them. When she had finished Tyler was quiet for a few minutes, and then he said, "Grandmother, I had no idea I was your heir. Did Uncle Julian know this when he sent me away?"

"Yes, he knew. But about a year or so after you left, I called my attorney and added him and his children in my will. You did know that he was disinherited by your great-grandfather, didn't you?"

"No." Tyler replied, astonished. "All Father said was that he was away and had been for many years. Why was he disinherited?"

"When he was young, about twenty or so, he started carrying on with this young girl whose father was your great-grandfather's best friend. In fact, they started the company

75

together, bought their first house and fixed it up and sold it. My father's friend, Samuel was his name, meant the world to him. They were inseparable. When my mother died in childbirth having Abby, he leaned heavily on Sam. Sam's daughter, Eliza, was only fifteen years old.

She became pregnant, but instead of marrying her, Julian ran off. Eliza committed suicide. She shot herself in the head. So my father disinherited him, but he and Sam's friendship ended right there. Daddy was quite angry. He pleaded with Sam, but Eliza had been his only child and the apple of his eye.

I found out much later that Julian had earned his living working for all kinds of companies. Shipping, engineering, oil fields. When he showed up here after your father passed on, I welcomed him and his family."

Tyler pondered all that she had told him. How could he not have known all about this? Because he'd been sent away as a child. Victoria smiled at him. "You're going to be rich one day. What do you think about that?"

He smiled at her. "I think that all the money in the world can't make up for what you and I missed. Are you sure you want to do this?"

"I'm very sure. It's what your grandfather wanted as well."

"Thank you, Grandmother."

"You're quite welcome. Now. Where is Ivory? I told her I'd meet her for lunch. We better do the interview here."

"I don't know where she is. She was gone when I woke this morning. I'll go look for her."

"Thanks, Ty. Tell her to meet me here at noon."

Tyler left, several things running through his head at once. He was going to be a multi-millionaire one day. His uncle must be livid. No wonder he'd wanted to get rid of him. He hadn't wanted the estate to go to him and thought by sending him away and keeping their letters from each other, the tie would be broken and his grandmother would choose another heir.

But she hadn't. She'd kept him as her heir and made

provisions for the others. No wonder Julian had hated him and been so cruel. Instead of being grateful that he'd been welcomed back into the family, he'd removed the one person he considered a threat. And then there were the family jewels; necklaces, earrings, bracelets, rings, and other assorted jewelry that were made of diamonds, emeralds, rubies, and pearls.

It was all coming back to him now. His father had told him about the jewels being missing. Jason had said it was just one more of the palazzos mysteries. But Aunt Abby had found them. He stopped walking as a thought struck him. No! It couldn't be! God Almighty, he had to find Ivory.

Ivory was in the garden. She walked to the other side of the latticed rose bushes and saw that there was a secluded place inside where a table and two chairs stood next to a statue of a Venetian maiden with water flowing out of a small urn she held under one arm. The hedge encircled the entire area and different kinds of flowers bloomed inside the alcove.

"Ivory! I thought you'd be here."

She jumped and gasped, "Damn it, Ty! Will you at least warm me next time? You scared me half to death!"

He plopped down on one of the chairs. "Sorry. I have something to tell you that's very important."

"So tell me."

"Here?"

He looked around. The alcove was the size of a small bedroom. He leaned forward and spoke softly, "I think I know why my aunt was murdered."

Her eyes widened. "You do? Already?"

"Yes. I just came from my grandmother. I think Abby was murdered because of the Ashford jewels."

"The what?"

"Ashford jewels. They've been missing for several years, in fact, since my great-grandfather died, and Abby found them six months ago. I think someone, probably

Julian, found out about it and confronted her. When she wouldn't tell him where they were, he killed her or had her killed."

"My God, Ty. Do you know what you're saying?"

"Yes. I have no proof. But at least now we have a motive."

Chapter Thirteen

The interview went rather smoothly. The two women liked each other. Ivory didn't press Victoria for details she'd be uncomfortable revealing. She started with her grandfather, Victor, and her grandmother, Sara. Theirs seemed to be a perfect match. They had both come from middle-class families and had one son, Vincent. Sara had died of a heart attack and Victor had been in a fatal hunting accident.

He'd been in Africa and had died shortly after the incident. Vincent married a woman from a very rich and prestigious family in England. Her name was Annabel. Her family had been against the match but she married Vincent anyway, and soon he had his own property management business and did very well. Annabel's family had disowned her but she never regretted her decision.

She had Julian and one year later, Victoria. But when she gave birth to Abby there were complications, and she died days later. Victoria told her about the Ashford jewels and how they had been missing for several years but she said nothing about her sister finding them or Tyler's inheritance.

Ivory thought she probably didn't want Max writing about it. Tyler had said she wanted to keep their existence and location a secret. Ivory didn't let on that she knew and she didn't write any of it in her notebook. As for Abby Ashfords death, there wasn't much to say. Someone strangled her, but no one, not even the police knew why. Apparently there were no clues either.

Ivory wrapped up the interview, thanked Victoria and told her she wouldn't need any more information. Max had enough and she didn't want to tire Victoria. Afterwards, Ivory decided to go to the west wing where Abby had been found. No one used that part of the palazzo. Not the rooms upstairs, at least. Victoria had told her which room; the corner bedroom. Ivory went into the room cautiously. It was dark and the lights hadn't come on when she'd tried the switch.

As she was making her way towards the window, she ran into something on the floor and almost cried out. She bent down to touch whatever it was and felt a warm body. She did cry out then and stumbled back. Someone was on the floor. But they hadn't made a sound when she'd cried out. She moved forward and tentatively reached down and touched the body. She felt soft hair that was rather long.

The person moaned. It was a man's moan and there was something familiar about it. She backed up when he began to move. Ivory didn't know what to do. He moaned again and she heard him utter the word, "Shit!" and she stepped forward again. "Tyler? Is that you?"

She heard movement and thought he was trying to sit up. He moaned with the effort. "Yes, it's me. What the hell happened?"

"I don't know. I just found you here. Do you remember anything?"

"I think so. I was coming in here to see if I could find any clues to Aunt Abby's murder. But minutes after I walked in the door, I heard something and then I was hit over the head with a very hard object. I remember a lot of pain and then nothing."

"My God."

She helped him get to his feet and he swayed. She put an arm around him. "Lean on me, Tyler. We'll get you out of here."

She helped him down the stairs and to their rooms. As she led him over to his bed he mumbled, "I don't feel so good." and then he passed out.

Victoria called the family doctor and he examined Tyler. He was in and out of consciousness. The doctor told them he had a mild concussion but it was nothing to worry about. He gave him a shot and said he'd be out of it for awhile, but that he should be better the following day. Ivory remained beside Tyler's bed and wouldn't leave.

Victoria was pleased to see the young woman's devotion

to her grandson. She had dinner sent up to Ivory and would come up to check on Tyler from time to time. Tyler would regain consciousness periodically and start to mumble things, but nothing Ivory could make out. Finally she went to her room and dressed for bed.

When she returned to his room he was calling out for her. She went to him quickly and leaned over him as she spoke to him soothingly. He reached out and grabbed her arm and pulled her down on the bed as he said, "Stay with me. Don't leave."

So she lay down beside him, telling him she would stay and not to worry. As it grew later, she got sleepy so she grabbed the blanket that had fallen to the floor and covered herself with it. Tyler already had a blanket over him and he now appeared to be sleeping soundly. The light in the other room was on, making the bedroom dim but with enough light to see if she needed to get up.

But she soon drifted off to sleep, feeling quite comfortable, even if she was lying next to a man in his bed.

From time to time during the night, Tyler would toss and turn, saying things that were incoherent. Ivory did her best to calm him by speaking soothing words to him, telling him not to worry and that everything would be all right. Apparently it worked because he would stop thrashing about and fall into a deep sleep. Sometime after four in the morning, he went on to sleep deeply without waking up again.

Ivory was able to sleep then but her dreams were a bit unsettling. She dreamt she being chased through the palazzo by a dark cloaked figure, but she couldn't tell who it was. Finally she wound up in the very room Abby had been murdered in and the hooded figure kept coming closer. She could see a knife in his hand now.

A very long and sharp knife. It glistened from some unknown light. He was almost upon her. With her back to the wall she cried out, "Stop! Who are you? Why are you doing this to me?"

A deep voice filled her dream with, "It is the curse. The Palazzo Delegado curse. You must die just as the others have done for centuries! You must die!"

She screamed as the knife came down and plunged into her, and it took her a moment to realize that she was really screaming and that it had been a nightmare. Tyler was there next to her and had taken her in his arms. "It's okay, Ivory. Baby, it was just a dream. A very bad dream."

She held onto him as the effects of the dream faded and her breathing returned to normal. They were lying down and she had her head on his shoulder with his arms wrapped around her. She rested her hand on his chest. He spoke to her soothingly, "It's okay now. It's over. Just a nightmare, honey."

When she heard his endearment and realized she was in his arms, her body stiffened. Then she relaxed again. She breathed deeply and then said, "Yes, it was a nightmare. A horrible one. Someone was chasing me through the palazzo. Someone with a knife. A very big knife."

"Jesus. Could you tell who it was?"

"No, but when I asked why he was pursuing me, he said it was the curse of the Palazzo Delegado and that I had to die like all the others."

"Damn! I should never have told you about the palazzo's history."

"It isn't your fault. He cornered me in the tower room where Abby was killed."

He frowned. "The room where Abby was killed. We were there, weren't we? Someone hit me over the head."

She lifted her head to look up at him. His face was mere inches from hers. His hair covered the pillow underneath his head and at that moment he looked like the 'Viking God' once more. A very handsome 'Viking god'. "Are you okay, Tyler? You had a really rough night."

He grinned. "Of course I'm okay. I heard an 'Angel' talking to me, making everything seem okay."

"That was no 'Angel', Ty. That was me. I've been very

concerned about you."

"Like I said, an 'Angel' was with me all night."

He put his hand behind her head and brought her mouth to his and he kissed her. She was startled at first, but as his lips moved over hers she began to feel something she shouldn't be feeling. She tried to pull away as she asked, "What do you think you're doing?"

"Kissing an 'Angel'."

Then he flipped her over on her back, brought her arms up and held them down on each side of her head as he leaned over and covered her mouth with his in a searing kiss that seemed to send currents of electricity through her. She started to struggle and then felt his tongue moving lightly over her bottom lip.

Her body relaxed and she started kissing him back, tongue met tongue and all her resistance faded. The kiss deepened and instead of holding her wrists, he put one hand under her head as he ravaged her mouth. She didn't even realize that her hand had slid up his chest and then entangled in his hair. Ivory was lost in his embrace. She forgot all her reasons for not wanting to be close to Tyler.

She just wanted to kiss him and never let go. Want and need pierced through her and he took his mouth from hers as he held her very close, his face in her hair. "Damn, I've wanted to kiss you like this for so long."

And then his mouth was on hers again and she grabbed him by the shoulders as her body came alive. She'd never known such a feeling as this, such passion, such desire. As his mouth traveled down to her breasts she told herself she had to stop him, but when he pulled her nightgown off one shoulder she knew she couldn't stop him, didn't want to stop him.

He pulled the gown down further and she couldn't seem to keep still. He spoke to her, his voice husky with desire, "I want you, baby. I want you right now."

He took his pajama top off and then his bottoms and she saw all of him for the first time. He was beautiful. She couldn't move or speak. He went to rummage in the dresser next to the bed and then in the bathroom. She undressed completely so when he returned he stopped short when he saw her naked on the bed. His eyes covered her body and then met hers. Words were not necessary. He had found what he'd been looking for.

She watched him now as he put on the condom and somehow he made the act sensual instead of something necessary or clinical. She couldn't take her eyes off of him. His glorious hair fell over his shoulders and the sunlight shone on it. He said, "You're beautiful, Ivory, and your skin reminds me of your name."

He joined her on the bed and as he watched her, he began to touch her and she held her breath and then reached for him, running her fingers through his hair. "Kiss me, Ty."

He immediately did so and wrapped his muscled arms around her. Their tongues met again and passion consumed them. As he kissed her he moved to position himself over her, and started to enter her, slowly at first. She tensed and held him to her. "Tyler! You're driving me crazy!"

"Am I, baby?"

Finally he couldn't take it anymore himself so he thrust himself inside her and they both gasped. He thought he might have hurt her so he stopped and looked down at her. "Did that hurt, baby?"

She ran both her hands through his hair and replied breathlessly, "It will if you stop."

He needed no further encouragement. As he began to move one thought was uppermost in his mind; why hadn't he met her before? It seemed as though he'd been waiting for this all his life.

He'd had other women. What made this one so special? The only thing he could come up with was that they fit together perfectly. He'd never felt such chemistry before. As she clung to him they rode as one until together they reached their ultimate goal and it seemed to last forever, and even after they stopped it seemed to stay with them for a very long time.

Chapter Fourteen

When Ivory woke she was alone in the bed. Tyler was nowhere in sight. The clock beside the bed told her it was eleven. She must've dozed off again. No wonder. She'd never felt so relaxed. And this time she hadn't dreamed. Just a deep sleep. As she got up she recalled everything in vivid detail. They'd made love. So much for keeping her distance. But she didn't mind.

It had been a wonderful experience. A thrilling one, in fact. She went to her bathroom to take a bath. Ivory felt as if she'd dreamt the whole thing but knew she hadn't. Refusing to think about anything else, she soaked in bubbles and relived it all over again.

Tyler was in the library looking at some of the books he'd read as a child. He'd done a lot of reading when he'd been young. His father had taught him early in life. He didn't remember his mother much. She was content to let her husband raise their son. The library had shelves of books on all four sides with a long table in the center and had a huge globe of the world in its center.

When he'd been younger he used to spin the globe, wondering about all the places he'd learned to pronounce. And now as an adult he'd gone to many of those same places on one business trip or another. Memories of his childhood came back to him now. Good ones of his father, bad ones of his uncle. It was all so long ago but sometimes it felt as if it were mere months.

"Well, Tyler, you should be real proud of what you've accomplished."

He turned to see his uncle standing just inside the room. As usual, Julian was in a dark suit. He had impeccable taste. His silver hair was combed back perfectly and Tyler recognized his expression. He was angry. Tyler turned to pull a book from the shelf as he said, "I don't know what you're talking about, Julian."

Julian arched a brow, probably because he had addressed him as 'Julian' and not 'Uncle Julian'. Well, thought Tyler, he was a man now and he wouldn't address this man as 'Uncle Julian'. Julian closed the double doors behind him and went to sit on the chair in the corner that was facing Tyler. "Come now, I'm very sure you do."

Tyler snapped the book shut and replaced it. He turned to his uncle. "You're referring to being grandmother's heir."

"Of course I am!" snapped Julian, "You've been gone for years while I've been here taking care of everything and everyone! Where have you been, Tyler? Off doing your own thing!"

It was Tyler's turn to snap, "And why is that, do you suppose? You sent me away long ago and made sure I'd never come back! And now I know why."

"Do you?"

"But it didn't work, did it, Julian? I'm still the heir."

Julian glared at him. Tyler went on as he started to walk around the room, "Keeping our letters from each other was a terrible thing to do to a child. Did you think Grandmother would just forget me? Or did you hope she'd die before I could be found?"

"How dare you!"

"I dare easily, Uncle. You had no right to do what you did. And for what? Here I am. Nothing's changed. The years have meant nothing to my grandmother. She still loves me and I'm still her heir."

"How long have you known about all this, Tyler? When did she tell you about being her heir?"

Tyler stopped pacing and turned to him. "I see. You thought I left without knowing I was her heir. You hoped I'd never find out. If I had nothing to return to then I'd just stay away. Well, you were half-right. I didn't know about being her heir. I was too young to know any such thing. You sent me away before I found out. But you were wrong about me having nothing to return to. I had my grandmother. Money wouldn't have been enough to bring me back.

I have my own money. I went out and made it on my own without anyone's help. It was my grandmother that brought me back. When I heard about Aunt Abby I was concerned about my grandmother. She only told me about my inheritance yesterday."

Julian just looked at him shrewdly. Tyler sat down on a chair by the table and spoke in a quiet, serious voice, "Don't think you can intimidate me any longer, Julian. I'm no longer that child you were cruel to and manipulated. I'm not afraid of you. In fact, you matter little to me. I'm here for my grandmother."

"How long do you plan on staying?"

"As long as I want. God, you think you'd be grateful for the fact that she allowed you back at all."

Surprise flickered across Julian's face. Tyler smiled. "Yes, I know about you being disinherited. Grandmother told me that also."

"What else did she tell you?"

Tyler took out the pack of cigarettes that Max had given him. He lit one up with the lighter that was sitting on the table next to the oval ashtray. He inhaled and exhaled as he looked at his uncle through the smoke. "I know about the Ashford jewels. My father told me about them. Grandmother filled me in on the newest development. She knows where they are."

Julian was thoughtful for a moment. Then he asked, "Did she tell you where they were?"

Tyler leaned back in the leather chair. "Why should I answer your question? It isn't any concern of yours."

"The hell it isn't! Those were my father's jewels!"

"Yes, and your father gave them to your sister and disinherited you."

"Shut up about that! It was all just a misunderstanding."

"Right. Apparently the young girl you got pregnant didn't think so because she took her own life."

"I'm warning you, Tyler. Don't talk about things you don't understand!"

"What's not to understand? You ran out on her and shamed her father and ours."

Julian jumped to his feet. "Shut up, damn it!"

"Or what? You'll hit me over the head again? Someone should've told you. I have a really hard head."

Julian looked confused at this point. "What are you talking about?"

Tyler could almost believe he knew nothing about what had happened to him. Almost. "You or someone you hired hit me over the head yesterday."

"That's ridiculous."

"That's the truth. I was up in the tower room where Aunt Abby was murdered. Do you spend a lot of time up there, Julian?"

Julian looked at him for a moment and then frowned. "I don't think I like what you're implying."

"Too bad. I think you are the one responsible for what happened to Aunt Abby."

Julian sat back down. "Well, I think you've lost your mind. Abby was my sister. I wouldn't harm her. You're crazy if you think I would. I was fond of her."

"You are also fond of the Ashford jewels."

"But I didn't even know about them then. I only found out they'd been found yesterday when Vicky told me."

"So you say."

"And I know nothing about you being attacked. I've been gone since yesterday morning. I just returned about two hours ago."

"How convenient."

Julian sighed. "Listen, Tyler, I may be guilty of keeping your letters from Vicky and hers from you, and I had a hand in sending you away, but I'm not a murderer."

Tyler had been watching him. He sounded sincere. But perhaps he was good at lying. He asked him, "And I suppose you know nothing about what happened to my friend Max?"

"Who's that?"

"You know who it is. He was coming here with me to

do an interview with grandmother."

"Oh, him."

"Yes, him. He was attacked and was hurt so bad he couldn't do the interview."

"I know about the interview, of course. I advised Vicky against it."

"That's not all you did."

"You're blaming me for everything that happens around here! You have no right to do so. I loved my sister Abby and I've been taking care of Vicky and Abby as well as the family business. Maybe trouble just follows you around."

"So you're saying you aren't responsible for any of these things?"

Julian stood up as replied calmly, "I'm saying I don't have to defend myself to you and I don't have to sit here and listen to your accusations. I think it would be a good idea if you left. You are nothing but trouble. You always were. And that was why I talked Vicky into sending you away."

With that he left the room.

Tyler stubbed out his cigarette. Doubt broke into his thoughts. Julian had seemed surprised to hear about his attack. But this was crazy. He had to be responsible for all that had happened. And everything led back to the jewels. Abby, Max, his attack, everything. Julian was greedy and he wanted it all, no matter who got in his way.

Chapter Fifteen

When Ivory entered the dining room, she found Austin and Rochelle there, having lunch. Austin smiled at her. "Hi there."

She returned the smile. "Hi yourself."

Danielle came in and asked Ivory if she'd like lunch. She told her yes and asked for a cup of coffee as well. Austin said, "We haven't seen much of you lately. Have you been out exploring Venice?"

"No, I've been here."

"How boring. You should be seeing Venice. Have you been here before?"

"No. This is my first time."

"Well then, you must see the sights."

Austin looked at his sister. Rochelle was dressed in a lavender pantsuit with a crisp white blouse. Her wavy blonde hair was down about her shoulders today and shone in the light. She put down her fork. "My brother is right, Ivory. You really must see Venice. We were going into town today for a little shopping. Why don't you come with us? We'd be happy to show you a few of the sights."

Rochelle smiled at her and Ivory was amazed how her smile transformed her face. She was radiantly beautiful. Danielle brought her coffee. Ivory said, "I don't want to put you out if you have other plans."

Austin leaned forward and said, "You won't be putting us out. We can still do our shopping and show you Venice. Besides, it will give us a chance to get to know you better."

Rochelle spoke to her brother, "Perhaps Tyler won't want her to come out with us. After all, they are newlyweds."

Rochelle looked at Ivory and smiled. "Husbands can be so demanding. Mine was, right up until I divorced him."

Ivory took a sip of her coffee. She'd almost forgotten she was supposed to be Tyler's bride. "Tyler isn't demanding at all. We both usually do what we want."

"Really?" asked Austin in surprise, "That sounds unconventional. Don't you have to check with him first?"

Ivory put down her cup. "'Check' isn't exactly the word I'd use. I just let him know where I'll be and that's that. I've always been very independent."

Rochelle frowned. "Well, what happens if you want to do something and Tyler doesn't want you to?"

"We discuss it further until one of us sees reason."

"Which one of you usually gives in?"

Ivory smiled. "Neither one. At the end of the discussion we're both in agreement. Tyler is a very intelligent man, but I guess it depends on the situation. There's nothing wrong with giving in once in awhile, and especially if you want the other person to be happy."

Austin looked at her in amazement. "Wow," he said, "I want a wife like you."

"No, absolutely not! I don't want you leaving the palazzo."

Ivory stared back at Tyler in disbelief. "What do you mean, you don't want me leaving the palazzo? I think this role you're playing has gone to your head! You don't order me to do anything."

"Look, Ivory, it isn't safe for you to leave the palazzo. Look at what happened to your brother."

"I know what happened to Max and I know why. But I don't pose a threat to anyone. I'm supposed to be your wife. I went along with this because you said I'd be safe. And I am so I want to go with Austin and Rochelle."

"Are you forgetting that someone hit me over the head just yesterday?"

"Of course not," Ivory said in a clipped tone of voice, "But I need to get out of here for awhile. And I'm not used to being told what to do."

"I am responsible for your safety, Ivory. Max is counting on me and I'm not going to let him down."

"And Max would be the first to tell you I don't like being told what to do or where to go!"

They were in their rooms. Ivory had found him there after she'd left Austin and Rochelle. Tyler went to one of the windows and looked out. "Then I'll go with you, that's the solution to this. That way I'll be sure you're okay."

"No."

He turned to her. "No? Did you just say no?"

"That's right. I don't want you coming along."

Tyler asked angrily, "And why the hell not?"

"Because they invited me, not you. They want to get to know me better. I don't need a babysitter. I'm a big girl, I can take care of myself."

"But Max won't..."

"I don't care what Max has to say! Why are you being so obstinate? I only want to go out for awhile and I don't need your permission to do so!"

She went to the door as she tossed over her shoulder, "It's a good thing we aren't really married, Tyler Ashford, because you would make a terrible husband!"

She left then before he could think of anything to say. A terrible husband! Why? Because he cared about what happened to his wife? Or rather, Ivory? This was getting confusing. Was he starting to think of her as his wife? Damn it to hell! They were only pretending to be married.

Was he being over protective? No, he didn't think so. He was responsible for her safety. Why was she being so obstinate? It was some time before he realized that he hadn't gotten a chance to tell her about his conversation with Julian.

Rochelle and Austin were waiting for Ivory at the back entrance. When they saw her, Austin asked, "Well? What did Tyler say about our going?"

Ivory smiled sweetly and replied, "He said it was a great idea and to have a nice time."

As they walked out to the gondola Rochelle murmured, "Amazing."

As it happened, they did have a nice time. They managed to see quite a few of the sights as well as do some shopping. They went to the Palazzo Ducale, which was also known as the 'Doge's Palace'. Ivory was amazed at the intricate detail of the architecture. Inside was a museum of sculpture that took her breath away.

A guide wasn't necessary because Austin and Rochelle knew quite a lot about the palace. Rochelle informed her that the 'Doge's Palace' had been the seat of the Venetian government from the 9th century until the fall of the Republic in 1797. Ivory could tell that Rochelle loved talking about this subject. Her lovely face lit up.

She told her that besides being the 'Doge's' official residence, it had also been the center of the Republic, containing administrative offices, armories, council chambers and chancellery, courtrooms, and dungeons. The palace was a symbol of political stability as well as a testament to Venetian supremacy.

It was also a showcase for the art of Venice, as well as sculpture and craftsmanship. The palace had been built in the 9th century as a fortress and was Byzantine in style, a combination of Moor, gothic, and Renaissance. Austin interrupted his momentarily animated sister to put in that the palace had the finest gothic facades in existence, Verona marble supported delicate Istrian stone arcades.

He showed her this and she thought it quite amazing. The loggia and arcade overlooked the piazzetta, which demonstrated the majesty of the State. It was a gothic masterpiece and Ivory didn't want to leave. There was so much to see. She bought a book in the palace's bookstore, which had more information.

Originally, Ivory had intended on asking Rochelle and Austin questions about their father, intending to learn something about Abby's death, but she was so caught up in what she was seeing that she forgot all about it. They showed her 'The Porta della Carta', which was the main ceremonial gateway, Rochelle told her, and it was named after resident archivists and clerks who copied petitions near by.

Above the portal was the sculptured figure of 'Doge Francisco Foscari', who actually commissioned the gateway. He was kneeling before a winged lion. Austin led them to the eastern wing, which held the courtyard. He told Ivory that there had been a fire in 1483 in this wing and had been remodeled to improve the 'Doge's' apartments and to provide grander magistrates offices.

Rochelle took over here, not content to let her brother tell Ivory everything. They were like two children who each wanted to reveal a long kept secret. Rochelle told her that the 'Scala dei Giganti', which meant the 'Giant's Stairway' was built in 1486 to provide access to the loggia on the first floor. In 1567 the staircase was lavishly sculpted with figures of 'Mars' and 'Neptune', which symbolized Venetian supremacy in both land and sea.

The 'Doge's' were crowned at the top of the staircase with a ceremonial jewel-encrusted cap. They went to the interior of the palace then and Ivory gasped. The vast ceiling was covered with large paintings bordered in elaborate gold frames. A frieze-border ran around the upper walls and featured the first seventy-six doge's.

Rochelle pointed out the 'State Inquisitors' rooms, torture chamber and prison. Under the eaves of the Palace was where Casanova made his daring escape in 1755. He had been arrested on charges of freemasonry and denounced for 'impiety, imposture, and licentiousness' by a spy of the 'Venetian Inquisition'.

Imprisoned in the 'Leads', the lofts of the 'Doge's Palace', he managed an escape. He scaled the Venetian rooftops close to the 'Bridge of Sighs'. After he tumbled through a skylight into the 'State' archives in the ducal chancery, he disguised himself in a hat trimmed with Spanish lace, outwitted the doorman and took a gondola to 'Mestre' where he fought with a Venetian spy before reaching safety and going on to Munich and Paris.

From the tone of Rochelle's voice and her expression, she was very glad that Casanova had managed to escape.

The palace was filled with many things; A maze of alleys, secret passageways, and a feeling of mystery. Ivory wanted to stay longer but Austin and Rochelle assured her there was much more to see in Venice. Next they went to 'The Museo Diocesano di Arte Sacra', one of Austin's favorite places. He told her it meant the 'Museum of Sacred Art'.

It was behind 'Doge's Palace'. The Romanesque cloisters of the museum on the canal formed an oasis of calm amidst the bustle of the city. There were medieval sculptures from 'San Marco', as well as Roman and Byzantine statuary. Upstairs was the permanent collection of 'Mannerist' and 'Baroque' religious paintings, crucifix's, gold and silver 'chalices', and a 'crystal tabernacle'.

Once back on the gondola they followed the street called 'Salizzada San Provolo' east to 'Campo San Zaccaria'. En route were several restaurants, including the 'Alla Rivetta', an inn serving cuttlefish and polenta. When Austin paused to take a breath, Rochelle winked at Ivory and told her they were coming to 'San Zaccaria', a church that was graced by 'Conducci's' curvilinear façade.

Byzantine and gothic churches intermingled into a whole Renaissance spectacle. The church was founded in the 9th century and eight of the early 'Doge's' were buried in the crypt there. They went inside the chapel and Ivory saw three beautiful altarpieces. Rochelle told her they were from the 15th century. She saw another magnificent altarpiece and Austin told her it was Bellini's 'Madonna and child'.

As they roamed around Austin also told her that three 'Doge's' had been assassinated in the vicinity and that the adjoining 'Benedictine' convent had been a place for lascivious living. Noble women were frequently turned over to nunneries to save money on dowries. It was known that there were 'Libertine Nuns'.

The nun's parlor became a social salon. Men are still made welcome in the former convent. From there they went on eagerly to the 'Arsenale' which was located in 'Eastern Castello'. Rochelle and Austin showed no signs of growing bored or wanting to stop the tour. Ivory was glad. She was having a great time. Rochelle took her turn now by telling Ivory that the 'Arsenale' was the oldest dockyard and that today the site was mainly used as anchorage for battleships.

It was previously a forbidden zone and public access remains restricted. However, two ferries are allowed to pass through the naval complex. It is still a working base and a few officers could be seen from their gondola. Rochelle turned to Ivory and asked her if she wanted to see more sights or if she was ready to go shopping.

Since they'd been so generous with their time and information, Ivory told her she'd like to do a little shopping since it was getting rather late in the day. As the gondola turned towards the 'San Marco' section, Austin assured her there was much more to see in Venice. They couldn't possibly even touch the surface of it all in a few hours.

Ivory thought that Austin would rather share the sights with her than go shopping. Brother and sister seemed very close but they didn't seem inclined to talk much about themselves. Ivory supposed that being raised at the palazzo had taught them to be somewhat withdrawn. But they knew a lot about Venice and they seemed like intelligent people.

When Ivory had first met Rochelle, she had thought she was distant and cool. Like life just bored her in general. But today she had been different. Very informative, at least. Austin teased both women constantly as they shopped in quaint establishments. He made Ivory laugh and he eventually started to annoy his sister.

At one point she told him, "Leave me, peasant! You know I don't like to be disturbed when I shop. How many times do I have to tell you?"

Austin shook his head. "Shopping is supposed to be fun, Rochelle. You act like you're shopping for a funeral dress."

"I will be if you don't leave me alone! And it will be your funeral!"

Finally he wandered off and Rochelle said to Ivory, "Men just don't get it, do they? Shopping takes concentration. Do you like this, Ivory?"

She was holding up a lavender dress of Venetian lace. Ivory touched the lace. "Yes, it's beautiful. Very exquisite."

"Exactly. I see we have similar tastes."

Chapter Sixteen

It was already dark when they arrived home and when Ivory went to her room Tyler was nowhere to be seen. She supposed he was still upset with her. But she wouldn't have missed her day with Austin and Rochelle for anything. She'd had a great time. Not only with them, but seeing Venice as well. And she'd bought several outfits.

She lay down for awhile and when she woke it was almost time for dinner. Going through the clothes, she decided to wear one of the dresses she'd bought that day. It was dark red velvet with a black satin belt. It was simple in design but she liked the scooped neckline. There were several boxes up on a shelf above the clothes that were hanging. Probably shoes.

A green velvet bag caught her eye. It was shoved in between two boxes. Taking it down, she realized it wasn't an evening bag as she'd thought. It opened up like a pouch and was tied with a black satin ribbon. Something solid was inside. Curious, she untied the ribbon and reached into the pouch and pulled out a book of some kind.

It was bound in white satin with the letter A embroidered in red in the center. Opening it to the first page, she read the feminine words;

This Journal Belongs To Abby Ashford

My God. This was Abby's journal. But why was it here? In Tyler's parents room? She flipped through it and saw that there was writing filling some of the pages. Leaving the closet, she went out to the other room and picked up the phone and dialed Victoria's extension. When she answered, Ivory asked her to have someone bring up her dinner because she was tired from her outing and preferred to stay in her room.

Victoria said she'd send Danielle with her dinner and then told her that Tyler wouldn't be there either. He'd left several hours ago to visit Maxwell. Ivory was glad he went to see her brother but was surprised as well. Hanging up, she settled in her room on the bed after changing for bed. She wrapped the white silk dressing gown about her and looked down at the journal.

Ivory knew the journal was important. It could answer many questions, but for now she didn't want Victoria knowing about it. At least not until she read it first. There may be nothing informative in it. Regardless, she'd let Tyler decide on whether or not to give it to anyone else.

Tyler sat quietly beside Maxwell's bed. Max was asleep and had been for a couple of hours. Tyler didn't want to wake him so he'd gone to take care of Ivory and Max's hotel bill. They were there because of him so he intended to pay for their stay. After visiting with Mrs. Piero for awhile, he went back up to Max's room. He'd only been sitting there about twenty minutes when Max woke up.

When he saw Tyler he smiled and said, "Well, hello. How long have you been here?"

"For a few hours, actually."

Max sat up. "A few hours! Why didn't you wake me?"

Tyler smiled. "Well, I haven't been sitting here all that time. I went down and paid you and Ivory's bill."

"What did you do that for?"

"Because you're here on my account. Anyway, I didn't want to wake you."

"It would've been okay to wake me. And you didn't have to pay our hotel tab either."

"It's done."

Max lit up a cigarette and when Tyler did the same, Max's eyebrow rose. "So you are making use of the smokes I gave you."

"This is my third one, actually. I feel like smoking every once in awhile."

"But I've never known you to smoke in all the times we've been together."

"It must be the tension at the palazzo."

"That bad? How's my sister?"

"She's okay. We went as husband and wife like we discussed."

"Damn! How'd you get her to go along with that?"

"I have my ways."

Max studied him. "What exactly is your relationship with my sister now?"

"We're friends. We've gotten to know each other better. We share my parents' apartments. Right now she's a little upset with me."

"Oh yeah? Why?"

"I kind of forbid her to leave the palazzo today."

"You what?"

"I know, I know, she doesn't like to be told what to do."

"Hell, no, she doesn't."

"Well, that's too bad. I'm trying to protect her. Someone hit me over the head yesterday and I didn't want her leaving the palazzo without me."

Max held up his hands. "Hold on a minute. I have two questions. One, who hit you over the head, and two, why would Ivory be leaving the palazzo without you?"

"To answer your first question, I don't know who hit me. I was up in the room where Abby was murdered when someone hit me from behind. Ivory found me. I had a concussion but I'm fine now.

And in response to your second questions, Rochelle and Austin wanted to show Ivory the sights. But she wouldn't listen to me when I told her I wanted to protect her. She got angry and went anyway. I even offered to go with her but she didn't want me to. She wanted time alone with Rochelle and Austin."

"I'm sure she'll be okay, Ty. No one would harm your wife."

"How can you say that? They harmed me! And you!"

"True enough, but no one knows Ivory is at the palazzo

to do an interview. There's no reason to be threatened by her presence. After all, that was the reason you went as man and wife."

Tyler frowned. "I thought you'd take my side in this."

"There are no sides, Ty. We all want to find out what happened to your aunt. So how is everything else going? Tell me all about it. Have you confronted your uncle yet?"

"Yes, just this morning. I think he's the one who hit me over the head."

The journal began simply enough. Abby wrote down her daily routines and her life was rather uncomplicated. She was an artist and spent a lot of time painting the sights of Venice and Italy. She adored her sister but stayed clear of Julian. Abby disapproved of her brother. She thought he was too controlling and demanding.

There were several occasions when he tried to forbid her to leave the palazzo, but she wouldn't put up with his telling her what to do. She'd told him in no uncertain terms that she would go where she wanted, when she wanted, and he couldn't stop her.

Ivory had to smile at this. She would've liked Abby Ashford. The journal went back to several months before she found the jewels. She'd been searching for them for quite awhile and was very excited when she did finally discover them. Ivory read out loud:

"I can't believe I found them! I never thought I would. I thought them lost forever. I tried to think like Daddy to try and figure out where he'd put them. And then I came across the blueprints of the palazzo and bingo! It all came together! How very clever he was. I had no idea this place had secret passageways and panels!

I guess I should have known. This is a very old place and its history has been mysterious and even gothic. Several murders were committed here. All old places have secrets.

That's how the murders were accomplished and why many of them weren't solved. The scoundrels would sneak through a secret passageway. They must have somehow found out about them."

Ivory paused. Secret passageways! Of course. She should have thought of that also. Where were the blueprints now, she wondered? She continued to read out loud on the next page:

"Something is happening around here. Something diabolical. It's been a few weeks since I found the jewels and told Victoria about it. The other night I got up to take a walk in the garden and was at the top of the stairs when I fell and very nearly injured myself seriously. It still hurts a little when I walk just so. But the thing is, I felt someone push me down those stairs.

I'm sure of it. I've been down that staircase a million times and never once lost my footing. Someone deliberately pushed me. But who? Who would do such a thing? And why? It doesn't make any sense. Not at all. I know of no one who would wish me harm. I could've been killed. I didn't tell anyone of my suspicions.

Not even Victoria. I keep telling myself I imagined someone shoving me from behind. It was late. Perhaps it was an accident. Julian thinks I'm eccentric as it is. He'd probably laugh if I told him I thought someone wished me harm."

Ivory jumped at the knock on the door. Setting the journal aside, she went to answer the door. It was Danielle with her dinner.

Chapter Seventeen

Ivory didn't eat much of her dinner. She was too anxious to get back to the journal. She believed that what Abby had thought about someone pushing her was true. And like Abby, she didn't understand why. Could it be because of the jewels? But why would someone wish her harm because she'd found them?

She hadn't mentioned anything about anyone questioning her about their location. At least not yet. Going back to the bed, she picked up the journal again as she sipped her wine. The next two pages were blank. Then:

"I received a threatening note today. It was in my room on my desk. It told me to be careful because the curse of Palazzo Delegado has chosen me as its next victim. It was printed and not signed, of course. The curse of Palazzo Delegado! What nonsense! There is no curse. Just some unlucky occupants who probably asked for whatever they got.

What I can't figure out is who would leave me such a message. No one in the immediate family would, and the people who work here have been with us for a long time. I am very troubled. Now I know that I didn't imagine being pushed down the stairs. Someone is playing a sick joke on me. But who?"

Ivory took another sip of her wine. Who, indeed? Would Julian do such a thing to his own sister? But again the question; why? The next few pages were blank. After the fifth empty page there was another entry:

"I've been very ill. I haven't even been able to paint.

My stomach hurts terribly. I finally let Victoria call the doctor when it became almost unbearable. I couldn't stand it any more. The doctor took me to the hospital and pumped my stomach. He said I'd had an allergic reaction to something I ate. He didn't think it odd.

He said it happens once in awhile. It was probably an herb that some people had an adverse reaction to. It was from a plant. Victoria said she'd tell the cook not to experiment with any new herbs. Bettina, our trusty cook, assured her that she hadn't but that she'd be extra careful. Everyone acted like it was nothing, just something that happens.

Since no one else was ill they weren't too concerned about it. They think I'm just allergic to a spice. No more spices in my food. But I am concerned. I can't treat this lightly. I think someone poisoned me. When I returned home from the hospital I could tell that someone had been in my room. Things were moved in my drawers and on my tables.

Even my paint supplies had been gone through. They tried to cover their tracks but since I've always been very orderly, I know when something has been moved. Thank God my journal wasn't in the room. Before I got sick I started going to Jason's apartments to write. It's very peaceful there and no one bothers me or is even aware that I go there.

I keep my journal in Jason's desk. If I hadn't I'm sure my journal would've been found. I feel unsafe in my room now. Victoria can tell something is wrong but I tell her I'm still feeling the effects of being sick. I can't tell her about my suspicions. I don't even have proof anymore. They took the note they'd sent me. It was in my dresser drawer. When I got back it was gone.

I don't know what to do. Writing it all down helps me try to sort it out. But none of this makes any sense to me. I did consider Austin was the one doing this. He's always been a practical joker. But this goes beyond what he would do. He's a sweet boy and we often talk together and he makes me laugh. It can't be him.

I'm just grasping for explanations. Dear Austin would never push me down the stairs or poison me. I don't know how I could have even considered him. If it were anyone, it would be Julian. He's always trying to get me to stay at the palazzo. But to wish me harm? He may get on my nerves but he is my brother. And he hasn't been pestering me lately.

We've actually been getting along. I'm at a dead end. No one here could do such a thing. If no one is responsible then perhaps I'm just losing my mind or getting senile."

Ivory paused in her reading. My God. Poor Abby. But how could she be just imagining all of what had happened to her? This woman seemed to have had a level head on her shoulders. Not at all like someone to imagine such things. And these weren't little things. These were serious things. Deadly things. She continued to read:

"I received another note today. This one was left on my pillow. It said the 'Keeper of the Castle' was watching me. That I can't hide from the Keeper of Delegado Castle. The only way to escape the curse was to give the Keeper an offering. Not just any offering, but a certain, special one. I had no right to keep what the Keeper wanted.

If I gave the Keeper of the Castle what he wanted then the curse wouldn't touch me. I should be prepared to give the offering when I am beckoned to do so. The note was printed just like the other one. I now know what this 'Keeper' wants. It's the Ashford jewels.

That is the offering he wants. It could be nothing else. Someone found out that I discovered where the jewels were. The only person I told was Victoria and she promised not to tell anyone. I know she kept her word. How did they find out? I have no intention of giving anyone those jewels."

105

Ivory quickly turned the page and continued:

"I haven't received any notes lately and nothing unusual has happened, but I know it's only a matter of time now. I spend a lot of time in Jason's room. It's the only place I feel safe. I've started keeping my journal in the closet now. Just in case someone searches these rooms."

Ivory couldn't believe what she was reading. Poor Abby. She'd had no one to confide in. No one to help her. She must've felt so alone. So helpless. She held her breath as she continued to read:

"Well, it finally came. What I've been expecting. Another note. This one said it was time to give the Keeper what he wanted. The Ashford jewels would be the offering. They belonged to the palazzo, not to anyone else. I am to go to the west wing, the tower room on the second floor, and I'm to bring the jewels with me and leave them there.
I'm to go at midnight. And I will go. But I'm not taking the jewels. The jewels will remain in the panel. I found them in the 3rd bookshelf, behind a secret panel on the bottom shelf. I almost didn't find them. There's a button under the shelf that opens the panel. And there they were. I remember I was so excited when I found them.
Now I wish I never had. I'm going to wait for this 'Keeper' when he comes for the jewels, and then I'll know who's behind all of this. I'll take the revolver Daddy gave me long ago. I never thought I'd use it, but I can't take any chances. Whoever this person is, they are a danger to me and everyone in the palazzo.
It will all be over tonight. Daddy always said never to ask someone else to do a job when you can probably do it better yourself. He was right. I found out where the long

lost jewels were, and I'll find out who the 'Keeper of the Castle' is."

Ivory turned the page but there were no more entries. The rest of the journal was empty. That had been the last time she'd written in her journal. And that must've been the very night she'd been murdered. Revolver or not, someone had strangled Abby Ashford.

Chapter Eighteen

When Tyler came in, Ivory was having another glass of wine and was sitting in the chair by the bookshelves. When he saw her he said, "Good evening."

The look on her face told him something was wrong. Her mind was still on Abby and what had happened to her. Tyler sat down on one of the chairs and sighed. "Don't tell me you're still upset with me?"

She hesitated and then replied, "I'm not."

"Then what is it?"

She looked at him for a moment and didn't know what to say.

"Ivory?"

"I found your Aunt Abby's journal."

He looked surprised. "You did? Where?"

"Up in the closet."

"And did you read it?"

She nodded. He asked, "What did you read that has you upset?"

"I read about it all, Tyler. Her finding the jewels, where they are, and about the events leading up to her murder. She was threatened long before she was killed."

"What do you mean? Grandmother never mentioned any threats."

"She didn't know. Abby didn't tell anyone."

"My God. Where is the journal?"

Ivory reached into the chair and pulled the journal out from beside her and handed it to him. He took it as he asked with a frown, "Who did it, Ivory? Who murdered my aunt?"

"It doesn't reveal that, Ty. Her last entry was before she met him in the tower room. Read it. It's all there."

"But why was her journal here?"

"She felt safe here. She hid it so no one could find it."

"Jesus. Poor Abby. Why didn't she tell anyone?"

"She didn't think anyone would believe her."

He opened the journal with shaking hands. Ivory sat there as he read. She saw all the emotions flicker across his face. But he didn't look up at her once. His eyes remained on the words his aunt had written. When he had finished he snapped the book closed and tossed it on the coffee table. But he still didn't look at her.

He gazed towards the windows and she knew he was seeing it all in his head. Just as she had until he'd walked in the door. Ivory had no idea how long they sat there like that. It was late. Nearly midnight. She didn't know what to say to him. It was best to let it all sink in.

The journal had shaken her to the core and she hadn't even known Abby Ashford. How much more devastating it must be for Tyler, who'd known and loved her. Her heart went out to him and she wanted to go to him and comfort him, but what comfort could she offer?

"Pour me a drink, would you, Ivory? And make it a strong one."

She did. Straight whiskey. He stood up and came to take it from her, but again he avoided looking at her. She could only imagine what he was going through. Now was not the time for words. He began to pace the room. Going from the windows to circle the room as his thoughts whirled around in his head.

He set the now empty glass down on the coffee table and then he finally looked at her. He didn't speak but went over to her and held out his hand. She looked at it and very slowly placed her hand in his. His fingers closed around her hand lightly and he slowly pulled her to her feet. He went towards the bedroom, still holding her hand lightly and she followed him.

Once inside the room he turned and pulled her into his arms, again very slowly. She went into his arms and held him with her face resting against his chest. He ran a hand over her hair and then took her by the shoulders to set her from him a little. He looked down at her and it was somehow communicated between them that no words were to be spoken.

He gently pulled her to him again and his mouth covered hers and that's where the gentleness ended. His mouth devoured hers in a searing, scorching kiss and she responded immediately. His hands were rough on her now, his fingers going through her hair. They continued kissing as hunger and need enveloped them. In one swift movement her gown fell off her shoulders and he touched her naked body.

She moaned now and he took off his clothes hastily, went into the bathroom for a moment, and then went over to her and they fell back on the bed. She reached down and grasped him in a firm hold and he all but growled. He pinned her to the mattress and entered her as he held her to him.

Their lovemaking was not gentle. It was urgent and passionate and powerful. When they cried out together they both knew this had been the only way to comfort each other. This had been what they needed. Both of them fell asleep afterwards. No words had been spoken.

And after a couple of hours, Tyler took her again the same way and she welcomed him. Towards dawn they reached out for each other again but this time it wasn't as volatile. He held her tenderly.

In the morning they woke in each other's arms. When Ivory opened her eyes she saw that Tyler was already awake. He looked down at her and smiled. "Good morning."

"Good morning, Tyler."

They didn't move. Her head was on his shoulder and his arm was around her. Finally he spoke, "This is nice."

"What is?"

"Waking up with you."

She didn't reply but smiled to herself. He sighed then. "There's a murderer in the palazzo."

She waited for him to say something else, but when he didn't she speculated, "Perhaps not. Someone could have come in through one of the secret passageways."

"No one knew of the jewels."

"Someone did." she reminded him.

He released her to sit up and she did likewise, pulling the blanket up over her as Tyler said, "It has to be Julian. Somehow he found out about the jewels."

"But you said when he confronted you it seemed as though he'd just found out himself."

"He could've been putting on a good act."

"But why would he?"

"I have no idea but I know he's responsible for what happened to Max. He didn't want anyone here, especially a journalist. He said as much to me. And if he could do that then he could do much worse."

"But murder his own sister?"

"He's a greedy man, Ivory. He wants it all. And he thinks he deserves it."

They were quiet then, each lost in their own thoughts. Tyler moved to the side of the bed. "But we have no proof. Abby didn't get a chance to name anyone. She couldn't. He made sure of that."

He went into the bathroom and Ivory watched him. Such a fine looking man. She'd never thought she'd have such a man touch her, let alone make passionate love to her. But it was very hard to resist him. She loved being with him.

When Tyler came out of the bathroom Ivory was gone. His mind was constantly on Abby and what he'd read, but thoughts of Ivory kept intruding. Especially thoughts of last night. What had happened to his cavalier attitude towards women? Why was he constantly thinking of Ivory? She was unlike the other women he had known. Maybe that was why he kept thinking about her. Usually he left them and went back to his solitary life.

He couldn't leave the palazzo. Not yet anyway. And he didn't really want to. He'd spent too many years away from his grandmother, and it was nice to be home. It had been a long time since he'd felt he was at home. Hotels were no substitute. And at the palazzo he felt close to his father.

When Ivory walked into the dining room, Julian was the only one there. She wanted to turn and leave but he had already seen her. He smiled. "Good morning, Ivory."

She told him good morning as well and sat down a little ways from him. Danielle came in right away as usual and took her breakfast order. After bringing her coffee and leaving, Julian asked, "What have you been up to lately? I haven't seen you around the palazzo."

"I went sightseeing yesterday with Rochelle and Austin."

"Did you now. You couldn't have picked better guides. I taught my children all about Venice from a very young age."

"Yes, they were very informative. I enjoyed myself very much."

Julian put his fork down. "I've been wondering about you, Ivory."

"What do you mean?" she asked, trying to keep panic out of her voice.

He smiled and replied, "I mean you don't seem like Tyler's type."

"And what exactly is Tyler's type?"

"Oh, I don't know. Someone who won't want to settle down in one place. Tyler has been on the move since he was young. Don't you find that rather difficult? Never having a home?"

"I do have a home, Julian. I have a home in Redondo Beach, California."

"But surely you'll have to give that up now that you're married to Tyler."

"Why would I have to give it up?"

"Because, my dear, Tyler would never be content to stay in one place for very long. Surely you realize that."

"Maybe you don't know him as well as you think."

"Or maybe you don't."

Ivory was getting upset. This man was too arrogant.

112

But she couldn't let him get to her. She smiled sweetly and said, "I know all I need to know about my husband. As long as I'm with him, I am home."

He just looked at her. "You're very sweet and romantic."

She laughed a little. "I'm afraid you're wrong about that. I've always been a little pessimistic about romance. I usually live by my wits and not my feelings. I've also been accused of being too direct."

"Then we have a couple of things in common, my dear. But I can't imagine Tyler appreciating them."

"Sometimes he doesn't. I never said we had a perfect marriage and that there were no conflicts. But conflict can make life interesting, don't you think?"

He laughed out loud. "I like you, Ivory. I like you very much. It's been a long time since I've had a conversation with an intelligent and direct woman. I can see what my nephew sees in you, but I have to wonder what you see in him."

"I see a handsome, kind, intelligent man who has a good business sense and is exciting to be around."

"Why, thank you, wife." Tyler said from the doorway. They both turned to look at him. Oddly enough, Ivory wasn't embarrassed by what he'd overheard. He went to sit next to her. Julian immediately got up and said, "I'll leave you two alone. I've got work to do. Ivory, thank you for the interesting conversation."

After he left, Tyler asked, "Did you and Julian have an interesting conversation?"

"I suppose so. He can't understand why I married you. He thinks you can never settle down. He even implied that I'd have to sell my house because you could never be content to stay in one place."

Tyler was thoughtful for a few minutes. "Julian has never really known me. I don't like him getting so personal with you. Who does he think he is anyway? It isn't any of his damn business where we live or how we live!"

It occurred to Ivory that the two of them were acting like

they were really married. She had just defended Tyler like a wife. This was getting complicated. In fact, she could actually see herself married to Tyler. Good Lord, what was she thinking? Not wanting to think too much about this, she asked him in a quiet tone of voice, "Are you going to give the journal to your grandmother?"

"I don't know. I don't want to upset her. I think this would really scare her. I will give it to her, just not now. What do you think?"

"I don't know, Tyler. I trust your judgement."

He grinned at her. "So you think I'm handsome, intelligent, and exciting to be around?"

Ivory threw her spoon at him.

Chapter Nineteen

At dinner that evening Victoria announced to everyone that she was throwing a party in celebration of Tyler's return. Everyone at the table was surprised. Julian didn't seem too pleased at the news. He asked her, "Do you think that's wise, Vicky? People are still talking about what happened to poor Abby."

Victoria answered him in a determined voice, "Then it's time they started talking about something else. We haven't had a social gathering in a very long time. In fact, have we ever had a party here? Well, I say its high time."

Austin smiled. "I think it's a wonderful idea, Aunt Vicky. When?"

"This Saturday. That gives me a whole week to plan."

"This Saturday!" exclaimed Rochelle, "But that isn't enough time!"

"Of course it is," Victoria assured her, "I already have the invitations made out. I'm inviting a few respectable families, not all of Venice."

"I see there's no changing your mind," Julian said with a stern tone of voice.

Austin interrupted, "Ah, come on, Dad. Are you afraid to have a little fun?"

Julian looked at his son disapprovingly. Rochelle put in, "Austin's right, Daddy. You need a little fun. You never go out."

"That's because I'm busy working, Rochelle. The family business won't run itself."

"And it won't fall apart in a couple of hours either." Victoria told him, "Ivory is going to think she married into a very dull family."

Julian looked at Ivory in her simple blue dress and smiled. "We wouldn't want her thinking that. I'll go along with this and even attend if Ivory promises me a dance."

Tyler stiffened but Ivory smiled and said, "Of course.

I'd be delighted, Julian."

They held each other' gaze and Ivory was aware of Tyler's scrutiny and she was sure Julian was aware of it also. Rochelle broke the silence, "We can go into town tomorrow and buy ball gowns, Ivory."

Ivory smiled at her. "That would be nice, Rochelle."

As soon as Tyler and Ivory were in their rooms, Tyler snapped, "What in the hell was that, Ivory?"

She turned to him in surprise. "What are you talking about?"

"You know damn well what I'm talking about! I saw the way you looked at Julian! Do I have to remind you that he is a murderer?"

She glared at him. "You don't have to remind me of anything, Tyler Ashford! I was just being polite."

"Polite, my ass! Polite is saying thank you when someone passes you the salt! You were flirting with him."

"Don't be ridiculous. I don't flirt."

"Well, it was certainly a good imitation."

"Tyler, you are acting like a jealous lover."

He spun around. "I am your lover, Ivory. But I'm certainly not jealous."

Ivory stared at him. They were lovers. They hadn't talked about it but it was true. Hearing him say it out loud shocked her to the core. They couldn't be lovers. That meant involvement. She swore she'd never get involved with him or any other man. She snapped, "We aren't lovers, damn it!"

"What do you call it? Be very careful, Ivory. Don't say something you'll regret."

Her mouth closed. She had been going to say something she'd probably regret. Instead, she went to pour herself some wine. Then she sat down. Tyler was already sitting on the sofa. Ivory spoke in a calmer voice, "We can't be lovers, Ty. We hardly know each other."

He had also calmed down somewhat. "What else is

there to know, baby? I know you through Max and what you yourself have told me. And you know practically everything about me. You sure as hell know more than any other woman does. I know what you like in bed, and you know how to drive me crazy in bed."

"Tyler!"

She looked away in embarrassment. He went on in the same silky voice, "It's true and you know it. Our times together have been spectacular. Can you deny it?"

She forced herself to look at him. "No, I can't deny it. But that doesn't mean we're having an affair."

"What does it mean then? That we're just passing time by going to bed together?"

"Of course not. You make it sound so cheap."

"No, Ivory, you make it sound cheap."

She hesitated, bit her lip, and said, "I'm sorry, Tyler. I'm just confused. I never intended for this to happen."

"Are you sorry it did?"

She smiled a little. "No. I'm not sorry it did."

He went over to her then and pulled her to her feet. He put his hands on each side of her waist and asked as he gazed deeply into her eyes, "Do you want to stop, Ivory? Do you want me to stop touching you? Wanting you?"

She held her breath and replied, "What would you say if I said yes, Ty?"

"I'd say you're a damn liar."

Then his mouth closed over hers and she clung to him. When his mouth moved to her neck he whispered in her ear, "Tell me you want me."

As his lips caressed her earlobe she said, "I want you." He held her close and slipped the strap of her dress off her shoulder, as he unzipped her from behind at the same time.

"Now tell me you want to have an affair with me."

"Tyler, stop. I can't."

"Yes, you can. It's what we both want."

When his hand moved over her she grasped his shoulders.

"Yes, Ty. I want to have an affair with you. Oh God."

He pulled her down to the floor and hastily took off his clothes. As she watched him Ivory thought there were worse things than having an affair with Tyler Ashford.

Chapter Twenty

Ivory spent most of the following day with Rochelle in several different shops. Tyler had remained behind to help with some of the more physical preparations. Victoria had asked for his help and he hadn't wanted to refuse her. He hadn't objected to Ivory leaving the palazzo this time. He merely winked at her and told her to be careful.

Ivory had been thinking about him all day. Had she actually told him she wanted to have an affair with him? It was almost unbelievable that she could have said those words. She wanted to blame it on the heat of the moment but knew that wasn't entirely the truth. So now she had to face the fact that she really did want to have an affair with him. What in God's name was she doing?

The reasons for not wanting to get involved had flown out the window the minute Tyler had kissed her. She'd fought it. God, how she'd fought it. She'd been burned more than once. She thought she'd fallen in love with a man named Brian Kranston. He'd even asked her to marry him. She'd only been twenty-four at the time and ecstatic about getting married.

In the middle of planning the wedding, which was to be held in approximately six months, Brian had to take a business trip to New York. He'd been a corporate attorney and business trips were not uncommon. Brian was an attractive, sensitive, caring man who was often jealous and moody as well, but she'd loved him and wanted to marry him.

When he didn't come back from Manhattan as scheduled, she began to get concerned. There had been no answer at his hotel room. A week later a telegram came. It was from Brian, and in it he told her he couldn't marry her and that he wasn't returning to LA. He could've just left it at that, to Ivory's thinking, but he'd felt the need to confess all. He'd been seeing another woman for the past month, a woman he'd met at a convention in London some time ago.

He was in love with her and they'd been married two weeks previously, he just hadn't known how to tell her. He was very sorry and swore he'd never intended to hurt her. He told her she was a very sweet and charming woman and he was sure she would find someone else in no time at all. But Ivory hadn't found someone else.

She'd torn up the telegram and vowed to never put herself in such a situation again. And she hadn't. Not until Tyler Ashford had breezed into her life with his devastating smile and handsome face. She had trusted Brian. He hadn't seemed the type to do what he'd done. He'd never let on that he was involved with someone else.

He'd always been very attentive and spent a lot of time with her. It's true that he had been unexplainably moody, especially before he'd left for New York, but she'd thought he was just nervous about the wedding. Ivory hadn't had a clue and that was what had been so upsetting. At first she'd been angry since she'd already made some of the wedding plans, so she'd had to cancel them right away.

It had been a difficult time for her. She'd had to strive not to be bitter. Perhaps she'd never really loved Brian at all. But the fact remained that he'd treated he badly and she felt she had to protect herself from being that hurt and miserable ever again. Max knew all about it and had even run across Brian once in Miami.

He'd met him once before when the three of them had gone out to dinner. Maxwell hadn't been thrilled with the relationship. He'd told her Brian seemed a little possessive. Brian hadn't wanted Ivory going out with her friends after work anymore and he even resented the time she spent with Max.

So when he'd seen him on the street in Miami, he'd grabbed him, spun him around and hit him square in the jaw and said, "That's for what you did to my sister, you asshole!"

Brian had just sat on the ground looking up at him while holding his jaw. The guy with Brian had just backed up, raising his hands as he told him he wanted no trouble. Max glared at Brian one last time and then walked away.

Ivory couldn't help but feel a small sense of satisfaction when Max had told her about the incident. So all she'd had left was Max and that had been just fine with her. Maxwell would never hurt her and he was the only man she trusted.

Enter Tyler.

She trusted him as well. They hadn't known each other for a long time but somehow that didn't matter. He was a kind, dependable, trustworthy man, and she was having an affair with him. Her pulse raced whenever he was near and it wasn't merely his good looks. It was the way he was with her. So protective and considerate.

She knew a little about his track record with women. Knew there was a possibility that she'd wind up getting hurt. But she knew he'd be honest with her. No sneaking around behind her back. And unlike Brian, he wasn't moody or overly possessive. And his moments of jealousy over his uncle had been flattering, not annoying.

He only wanted to protect her. He cared deeply about her safety. Ivory wasn't used to any man other than her brother feeling protective of her. But she liked it. Ivory smiled. Excitement and passion had entered her life. She hadn't asked for it, but it had found her regardless of her unwillingness to accept it.

She was still skeptical. Old habits died hard. But there was a type of security she felt in being around Tyler. She could still be cautious and enjoy her time with him as well. It just goes to show you that life still surprises you whether you're ready to be surprised or not.

After several hours of helping his grandmother finalize the plans for the party, they had lunch on her terrace. Over tea Victoria smiled at him and said, "Thanks for your help, Tyler. I seem to be getting tired easily these days."

Tyler frowned in concern. "Are you okay, Grandmother? When was your last physical?"

"Last month. Don't worry about me. It's just old age.

I'm eighty years old, after all."

Tyler raised an eyebrow. He hadn't realized she was that age. He grinned at her. "You look sixty and not a day older."

She laughed. "Goodness, it's good to have you here. You make me feel young, Tyler my boy."

He smiled at her lovingly. She put her cup down, settled back in the high-back antique chair and asked, "Tell me, darling man, how do you like your new wife?"

He shook his head at her and admonished, "Now Grandmother, you know that Ivory isn't my real wife."

"Well, she certainly should be!"

She'd spoken with such certainty that he stared back at her, surprised. "Grandmother!"

"Well, it's true. I've seen the way you two look at each other. One would think you were really newlyweds."

"We're just pretending, nothing more."

"That's bull and you know it! Ivory is perfect for you and you are exactly what she needs."

"And how did you come to that conclusion?"

"I've spent time with her. I'd have to be deaf, dumb, and blind not to figure it out. I may be up in years but I'm not senile. Not yet anyway. Have you kissed her yet?"

He was really taken back then. He laughed and said, "I see you have no problem speaking your mind."

"Never did, my boy, never did. Answer my question."

He grinned at her and she hit the table with one hand, making the plates clatter. "I knew it! And dare I hope you two have gone a bit further than that?"

He looked away, embarrassed for a minute. He wasn't used to having such conversations with his grandmother. She exclaimed, "Good man! I knew you had it in you!"

He looked at her, trying not to smile. "Now Grandmother, I never admitted anything."

"Oh, I know, I know. A gentleman never kisses and tells. You don't have to actually tell me, Grandson. I see it in your eyes. You always did have very expressive eyes."

"I have a few business associates who would disagree

122

with you."

"Oh, I'm sure you're a shrewd businessman all right, but I know you, Tyler. I can tell that you care for Ivory."

He sighed. "She doesn't want to be involved in a relationship, Grandmother. She fights me all the way."

"But you won her over," Victoria said with assurance, "And she is in a relationship, no matter how much she denies it. And you, handsome man, how do you feel about relationships?"

"Well, I don't usually get involved either. Women have come and gone. I had a serious thing for a woman once, got burned, and never looked back. I've always been on my own. So has Ivory."

"Love em' and leave em', eh? Well, if you leave this one you are a fool. Ivory is worth keeping. She's beautiful as well as kind and intelligent. I couldn't help but notice last night how you squirmed when Julian asked her to save him a dance."

"Squirmed? Me? Grandmother, I do not squirm."

"The hell you don't."

"I just don't trust Julian, that's all. I think he's responsible for a lot of things that have happened."

"Please, Tyler, let's not talk about Julian. The subject depresses me. I want to talk about you and Ivory."

"Forget it. I'm not answering any more of your questions."

"You haven't answered any. I guessed."

"Whatever."

"All right, Tyler, but let me offer a word of advice. Marry her."

"That's two words."

"Whatever."

Chapter Twenty One

The days seemed to go by quickly and Ivory had never been happier. Tyler and her slept together every night and it was like paradise for both of them. No mention was made of Ivory's reluctance to have an affair. Most of her time was spent with Victoria, seeing to the final details for the party. The two women, young and old, liked each other's company.

Two nights before the party Austin and Tyler went into town to purchase their tuxedos. On her own, Ivory wandered into the library. She wanted to see the shelf where the Ashford jewels were kept. She felt under the shelf and found the button that opened the secret panel. However, she didn't open it. It was too risky.

Browsing the shelves of books, she was impressed by the extensive collection. She was so absorbed that she didn't hear Julian come into the room. He watched her for a moment. "Just the person I've been looking for."

She spun around. "Julian! You startled me."

"Sorry about that."

"Why were you looking for me?"

"Because, my dear, you are the only one whom I'm sure can give me a good chess game. You do play, don't you?"

She smiled. "Of course. Doesn't everyone?"

"Actually, no. I somehow neglected to teach my children the game. And they're always busy with something else anyway. How about it? Are you up for a challenge?"

She laughed. "Always."

"That's my girl."

He went over to a shelf in the corner and brought the game to a small table with two chairs by a window that overlooked the garden. They took their seats opposite each other and Julian started setting up the game. He asked, "Does Tyler play chess?"

"I don't really know. The subject has never come up."

"Where is he anyway?"

"Out with your son buying tuxedos."

"I see. The party is Saturday, isn't it?"

"It is."

"I know Victoria has been very busy with the preparations."

"Yes, she's very excited about it."

"It's been ages since we've had any kind of social engagement here at the palazzo. I guess it's because we feel so isolated here."

"Rochelle says you don't socialize much."

He made the first move. "No, my life is my work. And I haven't met anyone whom I'd care to spend any amount of time with."

She moved her pawn. "I know what you mean. Before I met Tyler I kept pretty much to myself also."

"You? I find that hard to believe."

"It's true. I used to go out with friends occasionally, but not very often."

"But why? You're a young and beautiful woman. You should be out having the time of your life."

"Let's just say the past hasn't always been kind."

"A man?"

"Yes."

"I too have wounds, my dear."

He continued to play. "Do you think we were wrong to shut ourselves off from life?"

She smiled. "Who knows? It's certainly more safe than taking chances."

She moved a piece. He paused and looked over at her. "But you took a chance in marrying Tyler."

"Yes, I did. Fate wasn't content to let me withdraw from life."

"Fate. You have a poetic way of speaking at times, Ivory."

"Thank you. So no one here plays chess?"

He made another move. "Vicky does, but she quit playing with me years ago. Said she was tired of always losing."

Ivory concentrated on her next move. After she made it, Julian said, "Good move, my dear. I see I'm going to have to watch more closely. You didn't tell me you were good at this."

"You didn't ask."

They laughed together. The game went on in silence for awhile. Ivory had always liked chess. Max had taught her when she was only ten years old. They played whenever he was in town. He was very good and she only managed to win once in awhile.

Julian was good also. She really had to concentrate on each move. After awhile Julian said, "I suppose Tyler told you that we don't get along very well."

"He told me."

"It's actually my fault. I sent him away when he was young. I never really understood him, I guess. I've made a lot of mistakes where he is concerned, Ivory. Things I can't change. And now that he's a man there's no way to bridge the gap between us. We're two different kinds of people. I don't understand or approve of his ways.

Never settling down. I thought he was irresponsible and would amount to nothing. I didn't want my children to pick up his ways. But I discovered on the Internet that he owns several lucrative businesses and is very well off. Imagine my surprise. But he never came back here to see his grandmother and I thought I'd never see him again. And now I find out he's married to a charming woman. But I still don't understand why he's never called."

"Well, he's here now, Julian. Isn't that all that matters? Maybe he was running for some reason. Or perhaps he didn't think he'd be welcome here."

"I guess that's it. Do you know how long he plans to stay?"

Was that the reason for this conversation? Was Julian trying to find out when Tyler would be leaving? She moved her queen and replied, "No, I don't. We haven't discussed it.

126

I know that he's enjoying being with his grandmother again."

"Yes, and so is she."

"Julian?"

"Yes?"

"Check."

He looked down at the chessboard and was utterly speechless. After trying to calculate all the possible moves, and finding there were none, he looked up at her in astonishment. "I can't believe it! I always win!"

"Not this time."

"My God! I'm in complete shock. I can't even recall the last time I lost at this game."

"Maybe you've finally met your match."

"Indeed I have. Ivory, are you gloating?"

"Of course I am. You are an excellent opponent."

"Again. We must play again. Maybe it was only blind luck."

"Blind luck in chess? Surely you jest, sir."

"Well, I bet you can't do it again."

"I bet you I can or at least give it my best try. Lay your money on the table."

"Fifty dollars says you can't beat me again, young lady."

"You got it."

"You're going to lose your money. I never lose a bet."

"Isn't that what you said about chess?"

He looked up at her. Then he laughed. "All right, little girl, I'm going to make you eat those words."

"Don't count on it, mister."

They played two more games and Ivory won both of them.

Julian and Ivory were laughing when Tyler walked into the library. "Am I interrupting?" he asked.

Julian said, "Tyler! Your wife beat the pants off me! Three times."

Ivory put in, "I won a hundred dollars, honey, look!" Tyler looked at the money in front of her, looked at Julian, and said, "Why do you think I married her? I plan on taking her to Vegas and cleaning up."

Julian laughed and said, "Smart man."

Tyler and Julian realized simultaneously that they were actually being civil to one another and even joking together. It left them both speechless. There was an awkward silence so Julian got up and said, "Thanks for the game, Ivory, and of course I want a rematch."

"Of course. I could always use the money."

They smiled at each other and Julian left as he said, "Goodnight, Ivory, Tyler."

Ivory told him goodnight but Tyler merely watched him go with confusion all over his face. And then he frowned. Ivory sighed. "Stop frowning, Ty."

"Why should I? You were playing chess and laughing with a murderer."

Ivory got angry. "Stop calling him that!"

He looked at her in surprise. She went on, "You might choose to not get along with your uncle, but I don't. I had a good time."

"Do you know what you're saying?"

"Of course I do. We had a nice time. And not another word about him being a murderer either! You don't know that for certain, and I'm finding it harder all the time to believe he could murder his own sister, jewels or not!"

"Ivory, don't let him fool you like he does everyone else."

"Ex-cuse me! I do have a mind to think with. Don't talk to me like I am an idiot!"

"I'm not. But I know him. I know how he works."

"How could you? You haven't seen him in years. Not since you were a child. I think he regrets what he did. He realizes he's made mistakes, Tyler. We all make mistakes at one time or another."

"Did he tell you that?"

"As a matter of fact, he did."

"Well, he's lying!"

"Lying? Why would he do that? He doesn't have to admit anything. Especially to me."

"I'm getting really tired of this, Ivory."

"Well, I'm getting tired of this conversation. Goodnight!"

She stalked out of the room.

Chapter Twenty Two

Ivory went to her own room and closed the door. Once in the relaxing tub she went over the evening. She had gone from being suspicious of Julian to actually liking him, and had enjoyed her time with him as well. She'd never seen the side of Julian that Tyler had. As a young boy, Tyler had felt frightened and insecure because of the way he had been treated by his uncle and then because he'd been sent off to a place where he had been surrounded by strangers.

That would scare any child. The memory of that time has apparently always haunted Tyler. But it had been a long time ago. And now, being back at the palazzo had brought back all those painful memories. Ivory could understand that. Unpleasant childhood memories always remained with you. She herself would have more bad memories if not for Max.

Their parents' death had been hard on both of them. But they'd had each other. Tyler had had no one. But he was grown now. Couldn't he try to put the past behind him? When he'd been a boy Julian must have seemed like a monster to him. But maybe Julian just hadn't known how to deal with Tyler. And perhaps he'd really been afraid that his children would be led astray.

On the other hand, she could also understand Tyler's point of view. He was sure Julian was responsible for what had happened to Max. And perhaps he was. The thought of a journalist at the palazzo had threatened Julian. The press must have been relentless over what had happened to Abby Ashford. Especially considering the history of the palazzo.

The deaths and strange happenings throughout the past were probably well known. To any 'reporter' it would make a good story. Julian wouldn't have known that Maxwell had no intention of exploiting the family. Victoria might have tried to tell him but he wouldn't have believed her. However, there was a huge difference in what he'd supposedly arranged for Max and murdering his own sister.

Of course, what had happened to Max had been terrible, if Julian really had arranged it. Max had really been hurt. But she wasn't so sure Julian had even been responsible. She had previously thought so because Tyler had been so certain. That had been before she'd even met Julian. Now that she had spent time with him she thought he was incapable of such crimes.

Of course, he could be putting on an act. It was entirely possible. After all, God knew she'd been fooled before. But why did she feel so at ease with Julian? At first, she'd been suspicious of him because of what Tyler had told her. Now she thought he was an intelligent, sophisticated, attractive man who'd made mistakes in the past.

Even what had happened between him and that poor girl who had taken her own life, could be blamed on his youth. He'd panicked and fled the scene. But it wasn't fair to hold the past against him. He had returned and taken over the family business as well as looked after his sisters and his own children.

Maybe she felt a bond with him because he'd been living the way she had, cut off from involvement because of bad experiences. He could be greedy and want the jewels for himself, he could resent the fact that Tyler was to inherit the majority of the Ashford estate. But could he be a murderer? Somehow she didn't think so.

By the time Ivory went to bed and tossed and turned for an hour or so she came to the conclusion that she had no right to tell Tyler how to feel about his uncle. After all, she was an outsider. Ivory was only there to help Tyler, not judge him. Someone had threatened Abby. Whether it was someone in the palazzo or not, no one knew.

She missed Tyler. Missed him beside her, touching her. She had no idea if he'd gone to his room or not. She hadn't heard him. Ivory had expected him to come to her room, wanting to continue their discussion. But he hadn't. He was staying away. Their argument had actually been rather foolish. They'd argued about Julian before.

131

From now on perhaps she should try to just stay out of it. She really should learn to keep her thoughts to herself. Maybe a visit to her brother was what she needed. Yes. Max could put things into perspective. He always did. She'd go see him tomorrow and tell him everything. Thank God for Maxwell.

"I think Tyler is right. Julian is putting on an act for your benefit."

Ivory stared at her brother. She found her voice after a minute. "Why would he do that?"

"Who knows? But I trust Tyler's judgement in this. Who else could've been responsible for what happened to Abby and I?"

"Well, I don't know but you don't condemn someone just because you can find no other suspects."

"I see you feel strongly about this."

"Of course I do. You've never met Julian but I tell you I don't think he's capable of murder."

"Why do you feel like that, Ivory? Is it because you have something in common with this man?"

She sighed. "Perhaps. I don't know. Don't you think it's possible that Tyler is wrong about this?"

Max shrugged. "Anything is possible."

"Gee, thanks."

"Well, Ivory? What do you want me to say? That this is all just The Delegado curse?"

"Of course not. I just want you to give me some advice."

"My advice is to try and stay out of it. You're there to help Tyler figure all this out and to do the interview."

"The interview is finished."

She reached in her purse and took out the notebook.

"Already? asked Max, "That was fast. How'd it go?"

"Fine. I didn't dig too deep. I like Victoria and I didn't want to make her feel uncomfortable."

"Understood. But now there's this journal of Abby

Ashfords."

"You aren't going to write about that, are you?"

He frowned at her. "Why not?"

"Because no one knows about it. Someone might figure it out."

"Don't worry, Ivory. I'm not even starting this story until you're gone from the palazzo. I'm working on something else right now and I'll be tied up for a year or more with two other projects."

Ivory relaxed. "Good. You will be careful, won't you, Max? I wouldn't want anyone to figure out what family you are actually writing about."

"I'm only going to use a little of what you've written and I always embellish. No one will know. Trust me. I won't even center it in Venice."

She smiled at him. "I do trust you, baby-doll. How are you feeling?"

"Better. I can get around easily now on the crutches. And I've been working."

"You have? What's the subject this time?"

"A football star and his rise to fame, along with him meeting the love of his life, an artist, who makes it big when she's finally discovered after years of struggling and being taken advantage of. Our football hero comes along and they fall madly in love."

"Sounds like a romance novel."

"It is in a way, but it's going to be my best yet. Speaking of romance, how are you and Ty getting along?"

Ivory looked at him with narrowed eyes. Max said, "Come on, Sis. You aren't going to actually tell me there is no romance between you and Ty, are you?"

She hesitated and then asked, "Exactly what has your best buddy been telling you?"

He grinned. "Nothing. That's why I'm asking you. So there is romance."

"Why do you say that?"

"Because I know you. You're too passionate about Tyler's reaction to his uncle."

"Well, I'm there every day. It's kind of hard not to get involved."

"I know Tyler and I know you. I can tell something is going on. Are you going to deny it?"

She sighed, leaned back against the chair and replied, "No, I'm not going to deny it."

"Then I'm right? That's great, Ivory."

"What's so great about it? You know how I feel about relationships."

"Oh, I know all right. So you and Tyler _do_ have a relationship? A romantic one?"

"To quote Tyler, 'we are having an affair'."

"You're kidding! You? And Tyler?"

She smiled at him. "Don't sound so shocked, Max."

"But I am shocked! I'll be damned. It's about time."

She frowned at her brother. "Aren't you the least bit concerned that I'll get hurt?"

"Not really."

"Why not?"

"Because of you and Ty. I think you're good for each other."

"You wouldn't say that if you could hear us arguing."

"Well, at least you are arguing. That's better than not getting involved at all."

"Oh yes, this is much better."

Max studied his sister. "Isn't it better, Ivory?"

She smiled. "Oh yes, Max. It's much better. Tyler gets me so angry at times but I don't regret a moment of it. I fought it at first. Really, I did. But he has a way of getting to me. I feel so alive when I'm around him, and I actually trust him."

"I'm so glad to hear you say these things. It's about time you entered life again and started feeling these emotions. I'm happy for you and Tyler. Don't worry so much, Ivory. Everything will be okay."

"If you say so."

When Ivory returned to the palazzo, tables were being set up in the small ballroom on the first floor in the east wing. It had previously been empty since there had been no gatherings held there in years, at least not since Victoria had lived there with Julian. There was a grand piano in one corner. As with all the other rooms, this one also opened onto the garden area.

Decorations were being hung and a bar was being set up along one wall. A huge stereo system was being assembled and there were people here and there, each doing a specific task. Victoria had hired extra help. And Rochelle and Austin were also helping out. Ivory walked over to Victoria, who was speaking to a young girl who'd obviously been hired to help serve the food from the long buffet tables, which were lined up against two walls.

The room was huge and the ceiling was adorned with encircling gold angels painted directly on it. The walls were covered in dark blue wallpaper with gold flowers. It was very elegant. A huge white stone fireplace was positioned in the far right corner of the room. Elegant crystal vases sat on the mantle with flowers in them. Roses, lily's, and carnations.

It was beautiful. Balloons and streamers fell from the ceiling and two huge chandeliers hung from the center of each side of the room. Victoria had finished talking to the young Italian girl. She saw Ivory and exclaimed, "Ivory! Did you have a nice visit with Maxwell?"

Ivory smiled. "Yes, I did. He's doing fine. It looks really nice in here."

"Doesn't it? This room is never used. At least not since my father died. But it's perfect for a party."

"Yes, it is. Where is everyone?"

"Well, Austin and Rochelle are with Julian in his office. They help him out with the business part time. And Tyler is working too, on his computer. He's in the library."

"Then I won't disturb him. Is there anything I can do to help?"

"Well, let me think. I'm not having the tables set up until tomorrow since the party isn't until six o'clock. You can have lunch with me, if you like. I've been running

135

around since early this morning and I need a break."

"That would be nice. I haven't had lunch yet."

They went to Victoria's apartment. She hardly ever ate in the dining room. Only at dinner with everyone else. After ordering lunch they sat out on the verandah and Victoria asked, "Will your brother be coming to the party?"

"Maybe, if he feels up to it. He's doing well but sometimes he's still in pain. He was actually hesitant to come considering how Julian felt about him conducting the interview."

"That's in the past now. Julian won't know who he is. There will be so many people here. If he's worried he can always use another name. If anyone asks we can say he's an old friend of Tyler's."

"I suppose that would be best, all things considered."

"It's a rotten shame we have to do this but I don't want Julian making the connection between you and Maxwell. He might get suspicious and come to the conclusion that you and Tyler aren't really married and that you are merely here to interview me."

"Would that be so terrible, Victoria?"

"Yes, it would. He'd be very angry. And I'm not sure what part he played in your brother's accident."

"Maybe he didn't play any part at all."

Victoria looked at her questionably. After a moment she stated, "You don't think Julian is responsible for any of the things that have happened. You like him."

"Yes. We've spent a little time together. I find it difficult to believe he could murder his sister."

"Then you disagree with Tyler."

"I have no business agreeing or disagreeing. What Tyler went through was terrible but I think Julian regrets it."

"Really? Has he said so?"

"In a round-about way, yes. He admits the tension between them is his fault."

"He admitted all this to you? He never speaks of it to me, ever."

Their lunch arrived and after Danielle left Victoria said,

136

"Ivory, you mustn't upset yourself over Julian and Tyler's relationship. There's nothing any of us can do. They are both very stubborn, each believing his viewpoint is the right one. They will either work it out or they won't. But enough of this. Let's have lunch."

Chapter Twenty Three

Ivory didn't see Tyler all that day. She knew he was avoiding her. At dinner that evening he didn't show up either. Victoria told them he was having dinner in the library while he worked. He was waiting for an important phone call. Rochelle and Austin were going to watch a movie in the den and asked Ivory to join them. It was an old Elizabeth Taylor movie.

She said she would and even Victoria joined them. Tyler hadn't been in their rooms when Ivory had gone to change for dinner. It occurred to her that she wasn't really helping in finding out what happened to Abby, and now they weren't even speaking. But what could she really do? What could anyone do?

Whoever killed Abby was either not in the palazzo or he didn't feel threatened by her and Tyler's presence. Perhaps he had given up on finding the jewels. And perhaps it had all been done by an outsider that had no choice but to give up his quest. It was a dangerous game this murderer was playing. After the movie Ivory returned to her rooms and found Tyler sitting in a chair near the windows.

The cool breeze blew the white lace curtains in and out of the room. He was smoking a cigarette and having a drink. He didn't turn when she came in. She closed the door after her and went to pour herself a glass of white wine.

"Where have you been, Ivory?" he asked while continuing to look out the window as he smoked.

She sat in her favorite chair by the bookshelves and replied, "When? All day or just now?"

He hesitated. "Both."

"I went to see Max today and then I was with Victoria for the rest of the day. Just now I was watching a movie."

"With who?"

"Victoria, Rochelle, and Austin."

He didn't say anything. Ivory sat there sipping her wine

for a few minutes and then said, "This is silly, Tyler. Why are you so angry?"

"I'm not angry. I'm tired."

"I haven't seen you all day."

"I've been working."

"So I heard."

She put the glass of wine down and stood up. "Look, I'm not going to sit here and try to pull a conversation out of you. I'm sorry we disagree about Julian. After all, I shouldn't be involved in this in the first place. I'm only here to help you. But I don't think you need me here anymore. I don't really think you ever did.

There's nothing I can do about the situation concerning what happened to Abby. There's nothing you can do either. Whoever killed her is gone or they've given up. I have no desire to argue with you. So I think that as soon as the party is over I should leave. You can make my excuses like we discussed. I will go stay with Max until he's better and then we'll go home."

He did look at her then. And he was angry. "You want to leave? Go ahead. But don't say I didn't need you here because I did. Apparently where you and I were heading was a little too hot for you. You never wanted anything to happen between us and your solution is to run away. So go ahead and run. I can't stop you."

"I'm not running away, Tyler."

"Then you've decided to end what we have, just like that? Because of a couple of confrontations?"

"No. That isn't why."

"The hell it isn't! Are you even going to say goodbye to my grandmother?"

"Of course I am."

"Julian will be heartbroken when he finds out you're gone."

"Keep Julian out of this. I've enjoyed my time here. I truly have. But this is your family, Tyler. My family is sitting in a hotel room all by himself."

"Say what you want, baby, but I know the real reason

you want to leave."

He got up and went to his room without saying another word.

Ivory went to her own room. What had just happened? Why had she told him she wanted to leave? She didn't want to leave, didn't want to say goodbye to him, but she'd gotten so angry the words were out before she even thought about what she was saying. But it was true. She wasn't helping him.

But to walk away and never see him again? What had she been thinking? My God. No. It couldn't be. She couldn't be in love with him! It couldn't be! But when she thought of life without Tyler she felt such loss and pain. How could this have happened? But she could no longer deny it. She was in love with him.

She would be hurt. Terribly hurt. Oh, why had she gotten involved in this crazy scheme to begin with? This was all Max's fault. Why couldn't he have befriended a fat, ugly old man with no personality whatsoever? Why was fate playing this cruel joke on her? Was God trying to teach her a lesson?

That she couldn't escape pain, no matter what? No matter how hard she tried to avoid it? But that was stupid. It wasn't God's fault. The blame was hers and hers alone. She should have never agreed to any of this. She should've refused Max from the very beginning. And she should never have kissed Tyler.

Sleep was almost impossible. Thoughts kept running through her mind, memories now. Memories of Tyler and her laughing together, in bed together, and even arguing together. But always together. And now she would be alone. Would always be alone. Eventually Ivory found herself crying. She'd found love only to lose it. No. Only to throw it away.

How sad. And she blamed herself. She could've been with Tyler. But no, she had to open her big mouth. Maybe it was better this way. Much better to end it now than to prolong the agony. She'd always felt that she wasn't meant to find love anyway. This just proved she'd been right all along. Ivory had been burned before, but it had never hurt so much.

She should've just stayed in Redondo Beach and never come to Venice.

Tyler paced his room, wanting more than anything to smash something, to hurl something across the room, but he couldn't bring himself to destroy anything in the room he'd had as a boy. There were black and white marble statues his father had bought him in Rome on the fireplace mantle. They were miniature statues of Zeus, Hercules, Athena, Adonis, Cupid, and Diana.

He'd always treasured the gods and goddesses. He couldn't destroy them, not even in his current state of mind. Of course there were vases as well. Intricate crystal and French glass vases that came from France, Greece, and Vienna. Forget it. He had never been prone to let his rage fly in the form of violence.

But damn it, he was angry. Frustration and panic gripped him at once, all but choking him. Ivory was leaving. She was leaving him. Was going to walk out of the palazzo and he'd never see her again. Oh, he'd see Max again he had no doubt. But never Ivory, he was just as sure of that. How could this have happened? And so soon?

He assumed they would eventually part. He knew she didn't want a relationship. But he'd hoped they would have more time together. Tyler stopped pacing and stood perfectly still. What was the matter with him? Why was he taking this so badly? He'd never gotten this upset before when he'd walked away from a woman. He was acting like a fool in love.

He continued pacing. No. That wasn't acceptable. He

was not in love. Not with Ivory or anyone else. He couldn't be in love. Wouldn't allow himself to be in love. Love was not in his vocabulary. Love destroyed people. Love equaled pain. He refused to be in love. It wasn't possible.

Couldn't be. Damn it to hell, could it be? He plopped down on the bed. He wasn't thinking rationally. If he just lay there taking deep breaths these emotions would fade away. They had to fade away. He already missed Ivory and she wasn't even gone yet. Well, it had finally happened. Something he never thought possible. Finally a woman was leaving <u>him</u>. So this was what it felt like.

Chapter Twenty Four

Just as Ivory had finished dressing there was a knock on her door. She'd overslept, having a disturbed night's sleep. She called out 'come in' as she ran a brush through her hair. She wasn't up to another confrontation with Tyler. Not yet. Not until after her first cup of coffee.

But it wasn't Tyler who walked in, but Rochelle, and she seemed very upset. Ivory had never seen her upset or even a little agitated. But she was agitated now. She closed the door firmly behind her and Ivory asked in a concerned tone, "What is it, Rochelle? What's wrong?"

Rochelle faced her. "I have to talk to someone and you are the only one I feel I can trust."

Ivory led her over to the sitting room area. "Sit down, please."

Rochelle did so. Rochelle was as elegant as ever in brown slacks and a cream-colored blouse with a lace collar. She wore her hair down today. Light blond curls fell over one shoulder. "I don't know what to do. Who to turn to. I'm going out of my mind."

"Tell me what's the matter, Rochelle. I've never seen you like this."

"I've never been like this. Not in a very long time and not in front of others. I've tried very hard to hide my fear."

"Has something happened? Why are you afraid?"

Rochelle looked up and her blue eyes revealed her inner turmoil. She said, "You must promise not to repeat any of what I'm going to tell you."

"Of course."

"I mean it, Ivory. Not to anyone. Not even Tyler. Do you promise?"

Ivory had to hesitate a moment before answering. "I can't really make that promise until I hear what you have to say. But I'll do the best I can."

Rochelle seemed to relax and leaned back in the chair.

"I'm sorry, Ivory. I don't mean to sound so unreasonable. It's just that I'm so frightened. I can't trust anyone."

"No one? Not even your brother?"

"No. I can't tell Austin. He wouldn't believe me. He never seems to take life seriously and he hates to be bummed out. But I'm in trouble. And I like you, Ivory. I feel we've gotten closer. I consider you my friend."

"I am your friend, Rochelle. And I want to help you if I can."

Rochelle took a deep breath. Then she reached in her pocket and pulled out a pack of cigarettes. "Mind if I smoke?"

"No. Let me have one too."

"I didn't know you smoked."

"I usually don't."

Rochelle handed her a cigarette. "They're French."

Ivory brought the glass ashtray closer. After Rochelle lit their cigarettes with a gold lighter she handed Ivory one and slipped the lighter back in her pocket and inhaled. Then she said, "Someone is going to kill me."

Ivory nearly choked on the cigarette. "What?"

"It's true. I've been getting these notes. Left in my room on my dresser. They're from someone who calls himself 'Keeper of the Castle.'"

Ivory gasped. Rochelle went on, "In the notes he tells me I'm going to die and that it's the Delegado curse. I think someone tampered with my food once because I started getting these horrible pains in my stomach. Like cramps. It was almost unbearable.

They finally went away when I asked Danielle to start preparing my meals separately from everyone else. No one else complained of these pains so I assumed someone purposely tampered with my food. Anyway, I've received these notes, three of them, within the past couple of weeks."

"Where are they now?"

"That's the odd thing. I had them in my dresser, hidden, mind you, and they've disappeared. I went to find them and they're gone. The first two threatened my life. Telling me I was being watched and that I couldn't escape the curse. He also said that Aunt Abby had died because of the curse and now I had to. But I don't want to die, Ivory! Not like Abby did! She was strangled. It's horrible!"

"I know, Rochelle. Try to calm down. I know it's hard. Did the notes say anything else?"

"Yes. And it's very confusing to me. He said that if I wanted to survive the curse then I had to give him an offering. Something valuable that would cause the curse to pass over me. In fact, the curse would leave for fifty years if I did as he said. But the really strange thing is that he wants me to give him the Ashford jewels.

He said to find them and bring them to the place where Aunt Abby was murdered. I'm to leave them there and not wait but go immediately back to my room. But I don't know where the jewels are. They were lost long ago.

After my grandfather died. What am I going to do, Ivory? I don't know how to find these jewels. I know Aunt Abby looked for them for a long time but she never found them to my knowledge. If I don't find them and give them to him he's going to kill me!"

Rochelle stood to her feet and put her hands over her face and started to cry. Ivory immediately went to her and put her arms around her. "It's okay, Rochelle. I'll help you. You aren't the only one this has happened to. I will somehow help you. We'll stop this madman."

Rochelle pulled away to look at her, tears streaming down her face. She wiped them away and asked between sobs, "W-What do you mean I'm not the only one this has happened to?"

Ivory caught her breath and brought her hand up to her neck. She hadn't meant to let that slip. She'd just wanted to comfort Rochelle. But this had all happened before. All of it. He was back. He hadn't given up at all. He had just chosen another victim. But why Rochelle? She didn't know where the jewels were.

Maybe he thought she did. Wasn't it more likely that he would go after Victoria? After all, they were her jewels.

145

Ivory sat back down, the enormity of the situation washing over her all over again. Reading it in a journal was bad enough, being present when it was actually happening was an entirely different matter altogether.

Rochelle sat down also and looked at Ivory in something close to mounting panic. Ivory couldn't believe she had let it slip. And now it was too late to take it back.

"Ivory?"

Ivory looked at her. "The same thing happened to your Aunt Abby."

"What do you mean?"

"The notes, the tampering with the food, and worse."

Rochelle's eyes widened. "But how do you know? You arrived after Aunt Abby was already dead."

"I know, but I found her journal and it was all there."

"Her journal? Where did you find her journal?"

"Up in the closet. Listen Rochelle, I wasn't supposed to tell anyone about this."

"Who else knows?"

"Just Tyler. He thought it best to keep it quiet. And now I've told you."

"But Ivory! You had to tell me. You had no choice. It's all happening all over again to me! How could you have kept quiet? Thank you for telling me. At least now I know I'm not the only one this has happened to. Did Abby give him the jewels? No, of course not. Otherwise he wouldn't want them from me."

"No, she didn't give him the jewels. She went to confront him and she took a gun with her."

"A gun? But the police found no gun."

"I know. He must still have it."

Rochelle paused and both women dwelled on their own tormented thoughts. Finally Rochelle asked, "Do you know where the jewels are, Ivory? Did Aunt Abby mention it in her journal?"

Ivory sighed and noticed their smoked cigarettes on the table. They must've fallen there when they stood up. How strange that she hadn't noticed. "Yes, Rochelle, I know where the jewels are."

"We have to give them to him! We have no choice. If we don't then I'm going to be murdered just like Aunt Abby."

Ivory looked up at her. "But how can we? The jewels belong to Victoria and who says it'll be over after that? This lunatic can't be allowed to get away with this. He's already murdered once. What's to stop him from doing so again?"

"But Ivory, he'll kill me! We have to give him what he wants! I don't want to die! Maybe he'll just go away once he has them."

Ivory attempted a reassuring smile. "I know you're very upset and terrified, Rochelle, but giving him the jewels won't solve anything."

"Oh yes it will. It'll keep me alive."

"Maybe not. Maybe he'll try to kill you anyway. After all, you know about him."

At the horrified look on Rochelle's face Ivory quickly said, "I'm sorry, Rochelle. I don't mean to frighten you."

"But you are! You're scaring me to death! You promised to help me."

Ivory bit her lip. Rochelle pleaded now, "Please, Ivory! Please help me!"

Ivory didn't know what to do. Rochelle was desperate and she had to help her. "We need to tell Tyler about this."

"No!"

"But he'll know what to do, Rochelle. He can help."

"No, he can't. We already know what to do."

Ivory looked at her helplessly. "Rochelle, I can't just hand over a fortune in jewels. They aren't mine to hand over. Maybe we should contact the police."

"No! If he's watching he'll know when we call the police and then he'll really kill me!"

"I don't know what to do."

"Save me, Ivory. Save my life. Aunt Vicky wouldn't want the jewels if they caused my death."

"I have to think about this carefully. If we have to we'll give him the jewels and then contact the authorities. He hasn't said when to give him the jewels, has he?"

"No."

"When he does we'll take it from there. Try not to worry too much. This should all be over soon."

"Then you will give him the jewels?"

"I can't answer that, Rochelle. I need time to sort this all out. I won't let anything happen to you. You aren't going to die if I can help it. But I will have to tell Tyler."

"But Ivory!"

"No, Rochelle, don't try to talk me out of it. Tyler is your cousin and he should know about this. I can't just hand over his family jewels without telling him first."

"But he won't want to help me. He won't agree to give the jewels up."

"Of course he will! How can you say that? Tyler cares about you. He wouldn't want anything to happen to you. Neither would anyone else"

"I don't know, Ivory. I wish you'd keep this between us."

"But why? Your family loves you. At a time like this we need to stick together."

"You don't understand. Aunt Abby probably didn't tell anyone because she knew they wouldn't believe her."

"Yes, that's exactly what she thought. Well, I don't know about the other members of this family, but I know Tyler isn't like that. You can depend on him."

"Ivory, just please think about not telling anyone. Promise me you'll think about it first?"

"Very well."

Rochelle stood up and smiled. "Thank you, Ivory. You have made me feel so much better. Thank God I came to you. I know you'll do what's best. This family has had enough scandals. We can handle this ourselves. There's no need to alarm anyone else. Let's just give him the damn things!"

She left then and Ivory took a shaky breath. So much for leaving the palazzo.

Chapter Twenty Five

Ivory thought about everything that Rochelle had said to her. It was all so overwhelming. And it had changed everything. Ivory could no longer think about leaving the palazzo after the party. She had to be there for Rochelle. But what was she going to do? Rochelle didn't want her telling anyone, but she had no choice. She had to tell Tyler.

She found him in the dining room having breakfast with Austin. He looked up when she came in and his eyes followed her as she went to the table. She said good morning to them and Danielle brought her coffee. Tyler hadn't spoken but he looked upset.

Austin carried the conversation. He spoke of the work he'd been doing for his father. Austin excused himself finally and left them with the prolonged silence.

Tyler pushed his plate away and asked abruptly, "So. When are you planning to leave?"

She hesitated and then answered him, "My plans have changed, Tyler. I won't be leaving right away."

He looked surprised. "Why?"

"I'd like to tell you, but not here. I don't want to have this discussion here."

"Surely you can tell me why you've chosen to stay?"

She put her cup down and her fork, even though she hadn't finished her breakfast. "Not here," she told him again.

He stood up. "Very well, Ivory. Let's go back to our rooms."

She followed him then, neither one of them speaking a word. She watched the way he moved as he went and admired the way he carried himself. His blonde hair fell back from his face and his look was very serious. Once inside their apartments he closed the door. She went to her chair and he pulled another one over to where she sat. She searched his face.

Such a handsome face, but oh so troubled at the moment. She didn't know where to begin. He looked at her and waited. She surprised them both by asking, "Do you have a cigarette?"

He reached in his jean shirt pocket and pulled out a pack of cigarettes. His shirt matched his jeans. He looked very masculine, very rugged. More than anything she wanted to reach out and touch him. Take his hand in hers, anything. But he seemed unapproachable. Like he wanted to keep distance between them.

And who could blame him? She wondered how he really felt about her leaving. He'd been angry last night. He'd accused her of running away. But today he was cool and aloof. He lit her cigarette with one of his own and handed it to her. She took it and inhaled. Tyler seemed to be searching her face now, his blue eyes a little confused.

He asked, "Have you decided not to run away, Ivory? Am I the reason you've decided to stay?"

"Not exactly."

He tensed and frowned. She went on, "Ty, this isn't about us. I don't want to get into 'us'."

"Then why am I here?"

"Because I have to tell you something. Something I've been asked not to tell you, but I've decided to tell you anyway."

"It would be nice if you made the least bit of sense." he said sarcastically.

"Don't start with me, Tyler. This is very important."

He ran a hand through his hair, frustrated, "All right then, tell me already."

"Why are you being so difficult?"

"Why?" he shot back sharply, "You ask me why? Because you're driving me crazy, Ivory! That's why. I don't understand you anymore. I thought things were going great between us and all of a sudden you tell me you're leaving. You're just going to walk away from what we have."

"What do we have, Ty? You've never really said. All

150

you've said is that we're lovers and that we're having an affair. Damn! I told you I didn't want to get into this!"

"But I do. Baby, I don't understand. Talk to me."

Her heart melted on the spot. Why did he have to talk like that? So sincere and caring. So sensual and pleading. She felt like crying. He must have sensed her state of mind because he stood up and pulled her into his arms. "God, Ivory, don't look at me like that. You have been tearing me up inside. I don't want you to leave. Not the palazzo and not me.

I want you to stay here. I want to wake up with you next to me. Don't you understand? I want you and I don't want to let you go. It would kill me to lose you."

She clutched him tighter and did start crying then. He pulled away to look at her face. "Oh God. Don't start crying."

"I can't help it."

She wiped her tears away and he pulled her to him and covered her mouth with his in a demanding kiss. It turned urgent and they clutched each other harder. In between kisses Tyler said, "I want you here with me, baby. Say you'll stay."

He kissed her again and afterwards she said, "Of course I'll stay. As long as you want."

"That could be for a very long time, sweetheart. You've done something to me, Ivory. I've never wanted a lasting relationship either. You think you're the only one who's afraid of getting hurt? But somehow, and believe me I haven't got a clue as to when, somehow you've become everything to me. I've fallen in love with you.

I can't deny my feelings any longer. I don't want to. I know you're scared. So am I. But we have to try and work this out. I want you more than anything. I need you more than anything. I never thought I'd feel this way. Love and I are perfect strangers, I assure you. Do you think it's possible that some day you might love me?"

She stared up at him, hardly believing the wonderful, romantic things we was saying to her. She replied, "I already do."

"You already do what?"

"Love you."

Shock flickered across his face. She smiled at him. "I admitted it to myself last night. I was so miserable, Ty. Thinking of never seeing you again. And finally I had to face the fact that I loved you. It wasn't easy. Do you really love me?"

He pulled her into his arms again. "Yes, I really love you. Me. King of non-commitments. It's such a relief to hear you say you love me. I was afraid you would never give me a chance."

He kissed her then and picked her up and carried her into his bedroom. And there he showed her that their previous lovemaking could not compare to now. This time they knew they loved each other and every touch, every feeling, every thrilling sensation was much more intensified because of it.

Some time later they lay side by side, breathing deeply. Ivory was so happy. So content. She couldn't believe that Tyler loved her. Then she remembered what she wanted to talk to him about. She sat up and pulled on her shirt. "Tyler, I have to talk to you."

He propped his pillows up under his head and smiled. "Isn't that what we just did?"

She reached over and ran her fingers through his hair and then touched the side of his face lovingly. "No, honey. What we just did was magic."

He grabbed her hand and kissed the inside of it. She shook herself free of his intense gaze and pulled away.

"What I have to talk to you about is very important. Quit distracting me."

"But I have to distract you. It's going to by my favorite thing from now on."

"Tyler! Pay attention. We have a problem."

He was more serious now. "What problem? I thought

we just worked everything out."

"We did, sweetheart. This is about Rochelle."

One eyebrow rose. "Rochelle? What about her?"

Ivory took a deep breath and then said, "I'm sorry, Ty, but I told her about Abby's journal."

He was even more surprised at this. He sat up and leaned against the headboard as he asked, "And I suppose you had a good reason for doing so?"

"Of course I did. It's happening all over again, Tyler. Rochelle has been getting notes from the 'Keeper of the Castle'. And she was poisoned also but she's better now. He's threatening to kill her. He wants the jewels. He told her to bring them to the tower room."

"Damn! I thought maybe this was all over."

"Rochelle is terrified. She pleaded with me to give him the jewels. She's terrified of dying. She didn't want me to tell you. But I had to. Rochelle wants us to handle this on our own, her and me, but I couldn't hand over something that doesn't even belong to me."

Tyler got up and started dressing. Ivory did likewise. She knew he was going over everything she'd told him. He ran a comb through his hair and turned to her. "Well, baby, there's only one thing to do."

"What's that, Ty?"

"Give the 'Keeper of the Castle' what he wants."

She gasped. "You can't be serious."

"But I am, beautiful. I'm dead serious."

Chapter Twenty Six

The party was in full swing when Ivory arrived. She was wearing a white gown with thin straps and a deep neckline. She wore her hair up in a French-roll and diamond earrings. No other jewelry had been necessary. When Tyler saw her he stared at her appreciatively. He was dancing with Victoria and his stare reminded her of the first time she'd seen him.

Across the room at another party and his look then had been as intense as now. He looked dashing in his navy blue tuxedo and white shirt. He was wearing a bow tie to match and she thought him the most handsome man in the room. His blonde hair was slicked back and she thought it gave him a European look. Austin claimed her first dance.

He was wearing a black tux and cream-colored shirt. He looked handsome as well. They chatted lightly for awhile and before long he had her laughing. Julian, also in a black tux, wore a pale yellow ruffled shirt and black string tie. He told her she looked gorgeous and she told him he looked dashing. Ivory danced with two other men, strangers, and finally Tyler took her in his arms.

"You look absolutely breathtaking, baby."

"Thank you, kind sir. And you look kind of delicious yourself."

"Delicious, huh? I like that. I saw you dancing with Julian. Somehow I didn't think he'd show up."

There was no anger or jealousy in his tone. Ivory smiled. "What? No snapping at me for dancing with your uncle?"

"No, now that I know how you feel about me I see no reason to get upset. And you know how I feel about Julian. But for some reason I can't bring myself to resent him as much as I did. After all, it was a long time ago. Anyway, I don't want to think about Julian."

"Do you think he's responsible for the notes to

Rochelle?"

"Even I have a hard time believing he'd threaten his own daughter. He would have to be completely insane. But then again, anything's possible with Julian. He could be mad as a hatter and pull it off."

Ivory shook her head but decided to drop the subject. At least Tyler had relented a little. That in itself was a miracle. They danced a few more times together and then went outside to the garden area. Tyler took her in his arms and kissed her. They were inside the alcove and no one else was around.

They kissed several times, each one making their hearts race and then Tyler put his hands on her waist and asked, "What would you do if I took you right here, on the ground?"

"You wouldn't dare."

"Wouldn't I?"

"Tyler Ashford, you are impossible!"

"Naturally."

He was leaning over to kiss her again when they both heard a female voice frantically calling them, "Mr. Ashford, Mrs. Ashford! Are you there?"

It was Danielle. Tyler called out to her and she hurried into the alcove. She seemed very upset. Tyler asked, "What is it, Danielle?"

"It's your grandmother! She's collapsed!"

"What! Where is she?"

"In her room now. The doctor's with her. She collapsed right on the dance floor when she was dancing with Mr. Julian."

Without another word he grabbed Ivory's hand and followed Danielle out of the garden.

They found Victoria in bed. She was wearing a loose nightgown of pink now. Someone had helped her out of her green ball gown. Julian was there by her bed as well as Rochelle and Austin. Tyler went over to her and Ivory had never seen him look so stricken.

Julian said, "She's unconscious, Tyler. The doctor said she had a heart attack. She was fine one minute and then the next she'd just collapsed in my arms. I wasn't saying anything to upset her. We were just talking about how nice the decorations looked."

Tyler took his grandmother's hand as he looked at her pale face. He spoke to Julian, "No one's blaming you, Uncle."

Julian just looked at him. There was no harshness to Tyler's tone. Tyler sat down on the chair Julian had just vacated. "She hasn't come around since it happened?"

"No," answered Julian, "The doctor's arranging for an ambulance. I better go and get everyone out of the palazzo. Come on, Austin, Rochelle, you can help me with the guests."

They left and Ivory went to Tyler's side. Tyler spoke in a strained voice, "Oh God, not this. Not now. We'd just gotten reacquainted. She should never have thrown this damn party. It was too much for her."

"I'm so sorry, Tyler. But maybe she'll be okay. She's a strong woman."

"But she's up in years, Ivory. She's eighty years old, for God sakes."

"Can I do anything for you?"

"Yes. Get me a strong drink, will you? I don't want to leave her side."

"Of course."

Ivory left the room. Tyler just looked down at his grandmother. Suddenly her eyelids started to flutter open and Tyler said, "Grandmother? It's me, Tyler."

Her eyes opened and focused on him. She managed to speak after coughing a little, "Tyler. My beautiful grandson. I'm going to be leaving you now. I'm sorry we didn't have more time together."

"You aren't going anywhere. I won't let you."

She attempted a smile but coughed again. He said, "Try not to talk, Grandmother. An ambulance is on the way."

She laughed a little. "Will that be a gondola ambulance? I've yet to see one of those. They must row pretty fast. And do they had a flashing light and siren?"

"I don't know. Julian just said the doctor had called for one."

"Silly boy. I don't think they're called that in Venice. I can't remember what they're called or the procedure for rushing a dying old woman to a hospital."

"You aren't dying."

"Of course I am, dear boy. I love you, Ty. I'm so glad I found you."

She squeezed his hand. Tears came to Tyler's eyes. "Please don't go. I need you."

Victoria swallowed with an effort and Tyler gave her some water. She grabbed his hand. "Tyler, don't sell the palazzo. Stay here. You and Ivory. The palazzo is our family home. It's part of me. Don't sell it."

"I won't, Grandmother. I swear I won't."

"Tyler, I hear your grandfather calling me. I have to go to him. I want to go."

"No! What will I do without you? Hang on. Help is on the way. I love you."

"I don't want help, dearest. I want to go. Remember me. Always remember me. I'll be with you forever."

And then, before he could tell her anything else, she drifted away and he didn't need to feel her pulse to know that she was with her true love at last.

Chapter Twenty Seven

The funeral was a quiet and sad affair. It was in Mirano, Italy, and to get there they had to take a boat down the coast of Venice. Mirano was just a few miles from the canal. They took cabs the rest of the way. Ever since Victoria had died the family had seemed subdued and saddened by her departure. Especially Tyler. He and Ivory were together every night but he didn't talk much and neither did she.

Ivory was remembering every conversation she'd had with Victoria. She'd liked her and missed her a lot. But her grief was nothing compared to what Tyler must be going through. She didn't press him for conversation. In fact, she hardly spoke to him at all. Leaving him alone was the best thing. When he was ready to talk to her he would. He'd spent the days after her death in the library, working.

He hardly ever showed up for dinner. Neither did the rest of the family. Julian had locked himself away in his office. It had been a very quiet household. Austin and Rochelle were hardly ever seen either, and for once Austin had nothing clever to say. On the day of the funeral they had quietly gathered together on the dock outside the palazzo and the ride to Milano had been done in silence.

They passed places that were very lovely but no one was interested in the scenery. Once in awhile Rochelle would say something quietly to her brother but not so anyone else could hear. The day after the party Ivory had found Julian alone in the garden. She'd told him how sorry she was. He merely smiled sadly and told her thank you.

Maxwell rode with them to Mirano. No one asked who he was. Rochelle had been instructed a long time ago to tell no one that Max and Ivory were related. Everyone assumed he was a friend of Tyler's but they were in no mood to entertain strangers. The funeral was a solemn affair and all eyes were on the shiny white casket being lowered into the ground.

The family had several gravesites and crypts reserved and Victoria was buried between her father and her husband. It was mainly ancestors who occupied the older crypts. Many flowers were left for Victoria and about two dozen mourners had attended the services. Victoria's attorney was present and he'd had a few words to say to Julian and then left.

Tyler was the last person to linger by the gravesite. As the others faded away, he remained. Ivory went with the others to give him privacy. Tyler bent down on one knee and took a deep breath. His voice was low and resigned when he spoke, "Well, Grandmother, I guess this is goodbye. I've always loved you. No matter where I was I thought of you. I will always love you and miss you.

It seems strange not to have you at the palazzo. I keep thinking I can just go to your rooms and find you there, sitting out on your terrace. But I guess you're where you want to be. Say hello to grandfather for me and father. Goodbye, Grandmother, and I <u>will</u> always remember you."

He joined the others after a moment and once back on the boat he took Ivory's hand in his. Max was sitting on the other side of him. Tyler looked at him and smiled. Max smiled back. To Ivory's knowledge the only words that had been spoken between the two men was when Max had first come to the palazzo that morning.

Tyler had thanked him for coming. Max must've sensed Tyler wanted to be left alone with his grief. After all, Max knew that Tyler had only come to the palazzo to see if his grandmother was okay.

Once back at the palazzo Tyler asked Max to stay the night. Max agreed, and Julian told everyone that Victoria's attorney, Mr. Darius, would be coming to the palazzo the next day for the reading of the will. No one said anything, just went their own individual ways. Tyler asked Danielle to show Max to a room. He would be in their wing, only he would be on the first floor.

As Max followed Danielle, Ivory and Tyler went to their rooms and once inside Tyler said, "I'm sorry I haven't been such good company, baby."

"Don't apologize, Ty. It's perfectly understandable."

"I'd like Max to move into the palazzo. There's no sense in him remaining at the inn. He will be quite comfortable here."

"Thank you. I'm sure he'd like that."

"Maxwell has always been a very good friend. We should all be together now. After all, I have him to thank for bringing you into my life."

He smiled at her. She loved him so much at that moment she felt like crying. He went towards his room as he said, "I'm going to lie down for awhile. I feel drained."

"Of course."

She went to her brother's room. It was very spacious and elegant. When Max saw her he said, "I could get used to this."

"Could you? That's good because you're going to get your chance."

He frowned. "What do you mean?"

"I mean Tyler wants you to move in."

"What? Are you kidding?"

"No."

"Wow. I definitely don't have a problem with that."

"Well, you might when I tell you what's been going on around here."

"You mean there's something else besides Victoria's death?"

"Oh yeah."

Max's room was very much like her room. There was a huge bed, dresser, and sitting area in front of the windows that opened onto the verandah. He sat on one of the chairs, pulled out his cigarettes and asked, "What now?"

The next morning Mr. Darius came and the family met him in the library. Ivory had lunch with Max on his

160

verandah. He looked out at the view. "How nice it is here. It doesn't seem right somehow that such horrible things have taken place here."

"I agree."

He looked over at her, his black hair ruffling slightly in the breeze. "So tell me about Tyler and you. You two seemed awfully close at the funeral."

She smiled. "We are, Max. As a matter of fact, we love each other."

"What?"

"You heard right, bro."

"So you're going to stay with him after this mess is over? You two are like a couple now?"

"Exactly like a couple."

"Man, is this good news. So what are your plans?"

"We don't have any yet. We've been kind of wrapped up in the funeral."

"Then this is a recent development?"

"That's right. I was going to leave after the party but Tyler told me how he felt. He was so romantic, Max. I never want to be without him."

"Wait a second. Is this my sister talking? Ivory Lawrence? The woman who has made a fine art out of turning men down?"

"Go ahead, laugh it up. But you won't be laughing when it happens to you."

"If it ever happens to me."

"Oh, it will. If it can happen to me then it can damn sure happen to you."

After Mr. Darius had finished he left papers for Tyler to sign, offered his condolences once more and left. Everyone sat there for a few minutes and then Rochelle and Austin quietly left. Tyler looked at his uncle. He must be in shock. Victoria had left everything to Tyler. The palazzo, the family business except for ten percent, which Julian owned, and the bulk of her estate except for the money she'd told him she was leaving to Julian and his children.

But the dollar amount of everything surprised Tyler even though he'd known about most of it. The family business was worth much more than he'd thought. Apparently Julian had expanded over the years. And Ashford Incorporated was doing well. Tyler lit a cigarette and his uncle took a sip of the brandy he held in one hand.

The silence went on and finally Tyler looked over at the other end of the table where Julian sat. Julian put his glass down on the table and looked at his nephew. "Well, Tyler, I can't say I'm not surprised. When do you want us to leave?"

Tyler frowned at him. "Leave?"

"Of course. You now own everything except for the money Vicky left my children and me. I know how you feel about me. I will leave and take my family with me. You can just forward my ten- percent of the profits. Everything you need is on computer disk. Apparently you have good business sense and I'm sure you'll handle the business adequately."

Tyler looked at his uncle for a moment. He'd never seen him so subdued. Julian asked, "Will a week be sufficient? That should give us time to pack up and to make other living arrangements."

Julian waited for his reply. He didn't seem angry or bitter. Tyler picked up his cigarette, inhaled, and looked at Julian through the smoke that filled the air between them. Julian started to stand as he said, "I'll take your silence to mean that a week is sufficient. I'm sorry about the past, Tyler. I was wrong about you.

Even if you can't forgive me, please try to understand that I was threatened by you. But it doesn't really matter anymore. You inherited everything anyway. I can't help the way I am. But I see now that I did my sister and you a grave injustice. I shouldn't have tried to keep you apart. She loved you very much. You can't know the regret I feel. But I will carry it with me always.

The mistakes we make in life can never be undone. I guess your wife made me see things a little clearer. She's a very nice woman. It isn't so much what she says, it's how she just listens and offers possible explanations for each side. Goodbye, Tyler. I will let you know where I am."

Before he could turn to leave, Tyler said, "Sit down, Uncle Julian."

Julian looked at him in surprise. He hadn't called him that in a long time. Julian sat back down. Apparently there was to be an argument after all. Too bad. He'd wanted to leave the palazzo in peace. Victoria's death had taken all the fight and resentment out of him.

Chapter Twenty Eight

Tyler sighed, put out his cigarette, and placed his hands in front of him on the table. "I don't want you and your children to leave the palazzo."

Julian looked as if he hadn't heard right. He asked in surprise, "You don't?"

"No, Uncle. This is your home. You, Rochelle, and Austin are welcome to stay here as long as you want."

Julian frowned. "I don't understand. I know you hate me. I would've thought you couldn't wait to get rid of me."

"I might have hated you once. But Ivory has gotten to me also. Made me see things a little differently. I've carried hate and resentment around for too long. I can't make any promises, but I'll try to forgive you for the past. I've made mistakes also. But you never had to feel threatened by me. I never wanted everything to begin with. This is very hard for me to talk about."

"I understand. It is for me also."

Tyler hesitated and then continued, "After today we won't bring the past up again. Maybe we can start over, you and I."

Julian smiled. The first smile Tyler had seen in a long while. Tyler said, "You'll have to be patient, Uncle. Childhood memories are hard to forget. But I need to know one thing; did you arrange for someone to beat up Maxwell Lawrence?"

Julian looked totally confused now. "Maxwell Lawrence? My God, is that who went to the funeral with us? The same man who wanted to do an interview with Victoria?"

"It is."

"You must've told me his name but I didn't connect the two. So that's the reporter."

"No, not a reporter. A journalist. He writes novels and articles. He wanted to interview grandmother to get an idea for a story. He takes what he finds out, uses part of it and changes the names, places, and circumstances so no one will actually know whom he's really writing about. He's very good at it too. You had nothing to worry about. Our family would've been protected. He wasn't out to cause a scandal or even embarrassment.

I would never have agreed to him interviewing grandmother if I thought he'd cause harm. He was really hurt by those thugs you sent. Max was just trying to help me get into the palazzo. At first I wanted to just come without anyone knowing who I was."

"But I didn't send any thugs, Tyler! Please believe me. I didn't want him here because I thought he was a reporter, but not enough to arrange for someone to cause him bodily harm. I wouldn't go that far. And I wouldn't murder my sister either, like you accused me of. I might've made my share of mistakes, but I'm not a murderer."

Tyler watched him as he spoke. He seemed truly upset and shocked by what Tyler had thought him capable of. He remembered Julian hitting him when he was a boy, but he'd never been vicious. When he'd hit him it had been because Tyler had cursed at him and said other horrible things. Striking him was inexcusable, but Tyler thought he'd probably asked for it in part.

Julian was telling him the truth. He kind of wished his suspicions were justified but no one was this good of an actor. You couldn't fake certain expressions and reactions. Tyler believed him. But then who was responsible? Who was the 'Keeper of the Castle'? He'd thought it was Julian until Rochelle had been threatened. He looked at Julian now.

"Maybe I've misjudged you also, Uncle. I thought you did it because of the jewels."

"The Ashford jewels. I can't say I didn't want them. When I was a boy my father always told me they would be mine. That changed when I ran out on the girl I'd compromised. I was scared. I ran away. But not because I was abandoning anyone. I knew my father would be mad. I intended to return and marry her. Once I thought clearer I knew I couldn't bring shame to her and her father.

What no one knows is that when I left I befriended this young man and we started hanging out with each other. One night when I was drunk I told him who I was. I bragged about who my father was and how well off we were. I guess I was trying to impress him. Well, he and some other young men knocked me over the head and took me to this abandoned house.

They were going to ask my father for a lot of money to release me. They beat me up pretty bad. When they were drinking one night they started fooling around and decided to beat me some more. Their plan was to send someone to my father to ask for the money. Their emissary had left before they started hitting me with this iron poker.

The kind used for a fireplace. I somehow managed to get it from one of them and hit him over the head with it. One of them had a revolver, so when he pulled it out of his pocket I knocked it out of his hand with the poker. I beat them with it then. I was really angry.

They'd beat me so bad I couldn't see out of one eye and my leg and back had dried blood all over it from where they had hit me repeatedly. But I left them half-alive and then tracked down the one on his way to my father. I must've been quite a sight. I found him in a tavern so I dragged him out and hit him over the head with the gun in the alley.

No one made a move to stop me. This all took place in Florence, Italy. I'd made it that far before I'd finally come to my senses. I took the note they'd written to my father from his pocket and I returned to Venice, but before I could get to the palazzo I heard about what had happened from a friend I happened to come across.

She had taken her own life and my child with her. I was shocked and angry. How could she have done such a thing? Why couldn't she have waited? But I forgave her immediately. After all, it was my fault, all of it. I shouldn't have run out on her. I never saw my father. I left Venice and didn't return until after he died.

Vicky welcomed me back. I never told her any of this. All she knew was that I had tried to come back but it had been too late. Once I had been somewhat successful in Europe, I married. I had a couple of businesses of my own. I owned a few pieces of property and hit it big in the oil industry. I traveled a bit.

Once back here I incorporated these businesses into the family business and put them under the Ashford Incorporated name. I brought my family here. I'd found out my wife had been cheating on me before I returned to Venice, but I didn't divorce her because of Rochelle first, and then Austin.

Finally she left me but up until that point she and I were miserable. I even doubted Austin was my son so I had a paternity test run. He is mine. I tried to overlook my wife's infidelities but after Austin was born she started another affair. I'm afraid I probably took out a lot of my frustrations on you, Tyler. I was unhappy and angry all the time.

All I had were my children and then you started to remind me of those young men who'd abducted me and beat me up so bad. I know it wasn't fair but I was afraid my children would pick up undesirable habits from you. You were such a wild and angry boy and I felt I had to protect them.

I also knew Vicky would probably hand the family business over to you and I'd worked so hard and I didn't want to see you destroy everything. So I talked her into sending you away and kept your letters from her and hers from you. I wanted everything that I'd been entitled to as a young man. The things my father promised me.

All I had was the business. After my wife left it really became my whole life. That and my kids. What happened to me always stayed with me. As you said, childhood memories are hard to forget. My marriage brought more bad memories which is why I felt I could never trust another woman.

I shut myself up in this palazzo and I tried to keep Vicky and Abby here as well. I only wanted to protect them.

Protect the family. My honor and pride was eventually restored and I wanted to make sure nothing scandalous or bad ever happened again."

Tyler just looked at him. "Jesus!"

Julian grinned. "I didn't mean to tell you all of this. I've never told anyone. But I guess I've kept it bottled up inside for too long."

"I'm glad you told me. It explains so much. What a terrible time you've had."

"Yes. I hope you believe me about Abby and your friend Max."

"Yes, of course I do. I believed you before you told me all this. And I've come to a decision."

"What decision?"

"I'm going to give you fifty-five percent of the family business instead of your mere ten percent. After all, you've built this business. You've worked hard to make it what it is now. I haven't. I have my own companies. I want you to continue handling the family business. Nothing will change. I will keep thirty-five percent because grandmother wished it. But the rest is yours, Uncle Julian. I'll sign it over to you.

We'll have to call Mr. Darius back to make it legal. And as far as the jewels are concerned, I'll give you half of them. I know grandmother and grandfather wanted me to have them, but I feel you are entitled to them as well. I'll probably sell my half. I think they're bad luck. I know where they are. Ivory found Abby's journal and in it she tells where they are located."

"You're being too generous, Tyler. Fifty-five percent of the company and half the jewels? Perhaps you should think about this."

Tyler grinned. "No, that won't be necessary. This is what I want. It feels right. Grandfather made his decision regarding you and so did my grandmother. Well, this is my decision. I've learned a lot today; about you and about the past. But most especially about myself. Will you stay here at the palazzo, Uncle Julian?"

Julian stood up, went over to Tyler, shook his hand, and

said, "Of course I will. And thank you, Tyler. Not just for the business percentage and the jewels. Thank you for listening to me and your willingness to try to forgive me. Do you think things will be different now? I mean, between you and me?"

"They're already different."

And then the two men embraced as uncle and nephew.

Chapter Twenty Nine

The minute Tyler walked in Ivory could see something had happened by the look on his face. "What is it?" she asked, "What's happened?"

He threw himself down on the sofa and stretched out his legs on the coffee table. She sat in the chair closest to him and waited. He didn't exactly look angry or upset. More like thoughtful and pensive. He put his arms back along the top of the sofa and said, "Things have changed, Ivory. A lot has changed."

"What do you mean? Did you and your uncle argue?"

"No, me and my uncle had a conversation. A very informative conversation."

"Really? Well, you don't look angry."

"I'm not."

He smiled at her. "Julian and I had a long talk. I no longer think he's responsible for Abby's death or even what happened to Max."

One of Ivory's articulate eyebrows rose. "You don't? Jeez, that must've been some conversation."

"It was. A real eye opener. I now know there were extenuating circumstances concerning the reasons why Julian was often cruel to me and why he sent me away. My grandmother left me everything. The palazzo, the family business, the jewels, and the net worth of it all was more than I'd thought. She gave Julian ten percent of the company and the amount of money I already told you about."

"Was Julian upset when he found out?"

"Actually, no. Once we were alone he asked me if a week would be sufficient time for him and his children to gather up their things and leave."

"They're leaving?"

"No, they're staying. I told him they could stay as long as they wanted to. I gave fifty-five percent of the company to Julian and also half the jewels. We'll make it legal when Mr. Darius returns."

Ivory stared at him.

Tyler laughed. "I see you're surprised."

"Very."

"Well, a lot of it is because of you."

"Me? What'd I do?"

"You made Julian and I see things from a different point of view. We need you, Ivory. I've already forgiven Julian for the past. We can start over now and be a real family."

"I don't believe I'm hearing this!"

"Well, hang on. You aren't going to believe the rest either."

He then proceeded to tell her what had happened to Julian all those years ago. He had Ivory's rapt attention.

Things were different at the palazzo. At dinner there was lively conversation and everyone just stared, speechless, when Tyler and Julian talked together about business and even joked with one another. Their laughter filled the room and the others just watched in something close to awe. Julian smiled at his children and asked, "What's wrong with you two?"

"Nothing, Father." Austin replied and continued his meal.

Rochelle was more outspoken. "What has happened with you and Tyler? I thought you two hated each other."

Before Julian could reply, Tyler said, "We're mending our relationship, Rochelle."

She looked at Tyler in disbelief. Julian said, "Tyler has graciously handed over fifty-five percent of the company to me."

Austin looked up. "Then we don't have to move?" Tyler shook his head. "That won't be necessary."

"Thank God!" exclaimed Austin with relief, "I didn't want to leave, but I was torn. I thought about asking you if I could stay on here after father left, but I didn't want to seem disloyal."

Tyler smiled at him. Austin said, "Fifty-five percent of the family business. That means father owns a total of sixty-five altogether. I must say, Tyler, I didn't expect that."

Julian put in, "Neither did I, son."

Tyler and Julian smiled at each other. Rochelle just watched them. Ivory noticed her silence and asked, "Rochelle, what do you think about all this?"

She looked over at Ivory. "It's better than dreading arguments all the time."

Ivory frowned. She'd thought Rochelle would be overjoyed. Perhaps her mind was on the 'Keeper of the Castle' and wondering when the next note would come. After dinner Julian and Tyler went to the library. Tyler had asked his uncle's opinion on one of his companies. Ivory liked seeing the two men get along so well.

Tyler seemed happy just as Julian did. She went for a stroll in the garden and eventually Rochelle found her there.

"Ivory, I want to talk to you."

Ivory was inside the green alcove. She turned to her. "Yes?"

"I wanted to ask you if you told Tyler about the 'Keeper of the Castle'."

"Well, Rochelle, he already knew about him from Abby's journal. But yes, I told him about you receiving the notes."

Rochelle looked upset when she said, "I wish you hadn't done that."

"But Rochelle, surely you see that your family is coming together now."

Rochelle paled visibly. "Tyler hasn't told my father, has he?"

"Not that I know of."

"Has he told him about Abby's journal?"

"I think he told him he knows where the jewels are, but not about the notes."

"So my father knows where the jewels are."

"I don't really know. I think Tyler just told him that he

172

knew where they were. Why, Rochelle? You seem upset."

Rochelle glared at her. "Of course I'm upset! You promised to try not to tell anyone about me receiving those notes and now everybody knows!"

"That isn't true, Rochelle. Only Tyler knows."

"But he might be telling my father right now!"

"Calm down. Do you want someone to hear you?"

Rochelle turned away and took a deep breath. Ivory said, "I told you I don't think Ty has told your father. He probably doesn't want to upset him. Their relationship is just beginning to come together. And if your father knew wouldn't he have said something to you already?"

Rochelle turned back around, relief on her serene features. "You're right, of course. My father would've come to me right away."

"Why don't you want him to know?"

Rochelle hesitated and then started walking around looking at the different colored roses and assorted flowers as she replied, "I don't want him to worry. He's very protective of me and he would want to call the police."

"Which wouldn't be a bad idea."

Rochelle turned to look over at Ivory. "It's a terrible idea. I thought we agreed on that."

Ivory sat down on the chair near the fountain. "I'm not so sure."

Rochelle walked over and sat on the chair next to Ivory. "What did Tyler say about it?"

"About calling the police? He didn't even mention it."

"What did he say?"

"He said there was only one thing to do."

"What?"

"Give the 'Keeper of the Castle' what he wants."

"Thank God."

"But there's something you should know, Rochelle. When he and your father started to work things out, Tyler told him he could have half of the jewels."

Rochelle looked shocked. "Why would he do that? Doesn't he realize that my life is at stake here?"

173

"Well, I think when the time comes, if the time comes to hand over the jewels, then Julian will agree to do so."

"But that means he'd have to know why!"

Ivory looked at her in confusion. Why was Rochelle so upset? Certainly she could see that everyone involved would want to help her. She watched Rochelle as she visibly got a hold of her emotions. Finally she smiled a little.

"I'm terribly sorry, Ivory. I just get so upset when I think of this whole thing. I'm really scared. I don't want my father to be involved. If he is then his life might be in danger."

"I hadn't thought of that. As a matter of fact, all of our lives are in danger. But I'll speak to Tyler. I'll suggest he not bring Julian into this until it's all over. The less people who know about this the better."

"Thank you, Ivory. I knew I could depend on you."

That night after dinner Tyler told Ivory he had some work to finish. So she went to their apartments and got ready for bed. When she'd gone shopping for the ball gown she'd picked up something special for 'Tyler's eyes' only. It was a black lace teddy with a long matching negligée'. She smiled when she saw how much the teddy revealed. As she was brushing her hair she heard Tyler come in.

She put the hairbrush down and went into the other room. When Tyler saw her he stood perfectly still. His gaze traveled the length of her and then back up to her face. "Wow." Was all he said. She laughed delightedly.

"I take it you like?"

"That's an understatement. Come here."

She went to him and when she was within reach he grabbed her by the waist, crushing her to his chest and kissed her deeply. As the kiss heated up she pushed on his chest and said, "Ty, I have to talk to you."

"Talk? You think I can talk when you're wearing that?"

She smiled. "Please. Try to restrain yourself for a few minutes."

"I think I might manage it for a few minutes."

He went to sit on the sofa, taking her with him by the hand. Once they were seated Ivory said, "I spoke to Rochelle."

"Don't lean over like that. You're about to fall out of that thing you're wearing."

"Tyler!"

She leaned back, drawing the negligee' over her. He said, "Spoiled sport. Okay, so you talked to Rochelle."

"Yes. She's worried that you're going to tell her father about the notes."

Tyler's face turned serious. "I haven't said anything to him yet but I really shouldn't keep this from him. He is her father."

"I know, Ty, but she doesn't want him to know. She's afraid it will put him in danger."

Tyler thought about this for a moment. "Maybe I shouldn't have said anything to him about the jewels. But I felt it only right to give half of them to him. They were supposed to be his originally."

"I understand your motive in doing so, but Rochelle is very afraid."

"I'm sure she is, but this nut hasn't left any more notes."

"You are absolutely convinced now that Julian has nothing to do with this."

"Of course I am. Rochelle is his daughter. He'd never threaten her. I just can't figure out who this guy is. I thought that maybe it was someone who had something against the family. I'm sure Julian has made enemies along the way. But it doesn't make sense as to why they would murder Abby instead of Julian himself."

"Maybe they just want to torment him. After all, this person doesn't know that Julian doesn't know about it."

"That's true, but how does he get in and out of here when he leaves the notes? Surely someone should've seen him."

"The secret passages. Maybe there's one that is accessible from the outside right into Rochelle's room."

"And Abby's?"

"There's one way to find out. Abby mentioned the floor plans, or rather the blueprints of the palazzo."

"That's right. How stupid of me. We need to find the blueprints so we know how he's getting in. Maybe we could even trap him somehow."

"That sounds dangerous, Ty."

"It is dangerous, but he has to be stopped. We don't want this happening again. What's to keep him from coming back and wanting something else?"

Ivory was quiet. Tyler looked at her and smiled. "I'll go to the library and look for them. But before I do, I wanted to talk to you about something else."

She looked at him in surprise. "What is it you wanted to talk to me about?"

"About marrying me, living here in the palazzo with me and perhaps starting a family."

She gasped. He grinned. "I see I've caught you off guard."

"Ty! Are you serious?"

"It's hardly likely that I'd joke about a thing like that."

"But. . . . . but. . . . . . ."

"Yes? Spit it out."

"But I didn't think you wanted to settle down!"

"And how did you come to that conclusion?"

"Oh, I don't know, maybe because you never have!"

He laughed. "Just because I've traveled a lot and never wanted a serious relationship until now doesn't mean I wanted to live the rest of my life like that. I never found a woman I could trust, love, or want to settle down with for any length of time. Well, that's changed now."

Ivory didn't know what to say. He raised an eyebrow. "Well? Don't keep me in suspense. Answer my question. Are you interested in being my real wife?"

She forced herself to take a deep breath. "This has come as a huge shock to me. I had no idea you were even thinking about this."

"Isn't that what most people in love do? Get married?"

"Yes, but we aren't most people."

"Ivory, if you don't quit stalling I'm going to think we have a real problem. I want to marry you. I don't want anyone else. I love you. I want to live here in Venice with you and I want us to have a child eventually. I want everything I never thought I could have. The question is; do you want those same things? Yes or no. It's that simple. What's it going to be, woman?"

She smiled. "I love it when you get masterful."

"Well, I love it when you answer my questions!"

"Okay, okay. What a romantic you are. I'll marry you, Tyler Ashford. I'll marry you, live here, and have a family."

He stared at her in shock now. She laughed. "Well? I answered your question. Don't you have anything to say?"

"I'm so stunned."

"Didn't you think I'd say yes?"

"I don't know. I'd hoped you would but I was prepared to be turned down."

"Why? You know I love you. Why wouldn't I want to marry you?"

"Because I'm a jerk sometimes? Because we often argue? Any number of reasons."

"Are you trying to talk me out of marrying you?"

He laughed and pulled her into his arms as he replied, "Of course not. I may be a jerk sometimes, but stupid I'm not!"

Chapter Thirty

Ivory and Tyler couldn't share their news with anyone at the palazzo because everyone already thought they were married, even Rochelle. Except for Max. They found him in his room, working at a table. He looked up when they came in. It was the next day and he'd been up working since very early. Ivory said, "Hi, Max."

"Hello."

They sat on his bed, Max turned towards them, and said, "I'm going in to see the doctor later today."

Ivory frowned. "Is everything okay?"

"Sure. I'm getting this cast and the bandages around my waist off today."

"That's great, Max," Ivory said with a smile she reserved for her brother alone, "Are you still in pain?"

"It comes and goes. It all depends on what I'm doing at the time. I'll be a little sore for awhile but the doc says I made a speedy recovery. The quickest he's ever seen."

Tyler put in, "Of course. Can't keep a good man down." Max looked from one to the other and asked, "What's up with you two?"

"Well, first of all," Tyler said, "You should know that Julian knows who you are. Who you really are."

"Oh yeah? Figured it out, did he?"

"No. I told him."

Max raised a dark brow. Tyler went on, "As you know, we were able to work things out. I told you about it yesterday since you weren't planning to join us for dinner. But I forgot to tell you that I asked him if he arranged for your 'accident'. I don't think he did, Max."

"I know you are trying to get along with him now," Max said, "But you were so sure he was responsible, Ty. Why do you suddenly believe him? You hated the guy, remember?"

"I remember everything, but I believe him. I explained a little of our conversation to you. I don't know who is responsible, Max."

"But don't you think it's possible that he's lying?"

Tyler shook his head. "I don't think so. His reaction was too surprised and he seemed to be really insulted that I thought him capable of such extreme measures."

"Then who did it? Do you think it was unrelated to anything here?"

Ivory put in, "It could be, Max. There are that kind of people, you know. Were you robbed?"

"Yes."

"Then that might have been the reason. We all just assumed it was Julian."

"No. I assumed it was Julian," Tyler explained, "It all seemed to fit. One of them told you to mind your own business so I thought it had something to do with your interview with my grandmother. Oh, I don't know. Things are so different now. Julian's different and I'm different. I guess we'll never really know for sure."

Max lit a cigarette as he asked, "Is it okay with Julian that I'm here?"

Tyler sighed and stood up. "It wouldn't matter if it was okay with him or not. This is my palazzo now. But once I explained how you wrote about people he seemed unconcerned."

"Does he know Ivory did the interview?"

"No. I'm going to tell him tonight."

Max inhaled and suggested, "Maybe you should tell everyone tonight at dinner. And while you're at it, tell them that you and Ivory aren't really married. Get everything out in the open."

Tyler and Ivory looked at each other and smiled. Max said, "Oh-oh. Something's happened. Why are you two looking at each other like that?"

Ivory looked at her brother. "We have something to tell you, Max. It's the real reason we came to see you."

"Well?" inquired Max, "Don't keep a guy guessing. I have a pretty vivid imagination, you know."

Tyler sat back down next to Ivory, took her hand in his

and announced, "We're getting married, Maxwell."

Max just looked at them. Ivory said, "It's true. We are officially engaged."

"My God in Heaven! I can't believe it! *You* two? Mr. Can't-stay-in-one-place and Miss Hands-off-or-I'll-break-your-arm?"

Ivory and Tyler laughed. Max stood up and made his way over to them without the crutches. He shook Tyler's hand and hugged his sister. "I'll be damned! Congratulations!"

"Thanks, Max," Tyler said, "But I think you have a good idea. We'll tell everyone tonight that we aren't really married."

Max said, "That ought to make it interesting."

'Interesting' was hardly the word for it. Julian, Rochelle, and Austin's reaction was numb shock. Julian was the first to recover, "You were pretending to be married? Whatever for?"

Ivory answered him, "So I could come and do the interview for Max."

Julian frowned. "Do the interview? So you know Max?"

At this point everyone looked at Max and the man in question smiled and said, "Ivory is my sister."

More shock and then Austin exclaimed, "Your sister!"

Rochelle said at this point, "I knew they were related all along, but grandmother didn't want me to tell anyone. However, I didn't know that they weren't really married."

She'd spoken more to her father than to anyone else. Julian didn't say anything for a moment. When everyone looked at him he finally spoke, "My, this is a shock. So Ivory, you came to do Max's interview. Did you even know Tyler?"

"I met him when I came to see if my brother was okay. Tyler and Max have been friends for many years. I agreed to help them. Tyler was very concerned about his grandmother."

"So you two are merely friends?" asked Rochelle.

Tyler looked at her. "No, Rochelle. We're actually engaged as of last night."

They were really speechless then. Tyler said, "I hope this hasn't upset you, Uncle. I guess I should've told you yesterday but I was sidetracked by all that happened."

Julian looked at his nephew for a moment and then he said, "I'm not upset, Tyler. Just surprised. I don't blame you, really. You wanted to protect Ivory."

Tyler was the one surprised then. He was surprised that Julian knew his true motive for the pretense. Austin said, "But I don't understand why. . . . ."

"Drop it, Austin." His father told him, "It's over with. Tyler had his reasons. Let's leave it at that."

Austin stared at his father. "I'm surprised *you* want to leave it at that, Father."

"Why? We all know the truth now. It doesn't really matter. Tyler and Ivory are going to be married for real."

He turned to Ivory and Tyler. "Congratulations you two. Do you plan on living here?"

Ivory replied, "If that's okay with you, Julian."

"Of course it is. We can all be a real family. I find Tyler's business advice very helpful. So you'll give up your house in LA?"

Ivory remembered him telling her she'd have to do that because Tyler would never settle in one place. She replied, "I don't think so. We can stay there whenever we go to Los Angeles. But I can't imagine ever wanting to leave Venice."

Tyler said, "I own a Real Estate office there and an apartment building. We can stay at your house when we go to check on those things. I usually go to LA twice a year. Maybe when we go you can show me the sights."

Ivory smiled. "It would be my pleasure. Do you like football?"

"I love it."

"Then perhaps we can go to a game."

"Can I go?" asked Austin, "I'd love to see a football

game!"

Ivory smiled at him. "You can all come. It would be a fun trip."

"Yes," agreed Julian, "It could be. I have business there as well. A couple of car lots. I could even look into expanding the family business there."

"Sounds like a plan." remarked Tyler.

Max asked, "So when is the wedding?"

Tyler looked at Ivory. "The sooner the better as far as I'm concerned."

She smiled at him fondly. "I'm in total agreement."

"We can have the wedding here if you like."

"I like."

Then Tyler said on a more serious note, "Too bad grandmother isn't here. She told me to marry Ivory. I wish I could've told her the good news."

"She knows, Tyler," Julian said, "She knows."

Chapter Thirty One

Tyler found the floor plans to the palazzo and discovered several secret passageways. Small spaced walkways to get from one room to the other. He even found a couple of entrances from the outside. He boarded those up immediately. There were secret panels that opened into several rooms: Abby's, Rochelle's, the study, the kitchen, the small ballroom, and the parlor which was hardly used by the family.

They spent most of their time in the dining room, den, and the main living room. Tyler didn't bother sealing up Abby's room, but he did Rochelle's. There was no need to seal off the others because he'd made sure no one could get in from the outside. There were sure to be more passageways in the other wings but he'd only been interested in the rooms that were occupied day to day.

It had taken him most of the day to seal up the one's he had. Meanwhile, Ivory had started making wedding plans. She'd wanted to ask Rochelle to go to the shops to look at wedding gowns but Rochelle seemed preoccupied. Ivory knew she was thinking about when she'd get the next note. She wanted to comfort her but didn't know how.

She assured her that Tyler hadn't told Julian about the 'Keeper of the Castle' and that he had no plans on doing so until the whole incident was over. Rochelle seemed to relax a little as the days went by and nothing happened. She even volunteered to go shopping for wedding gowns with Ivory.

Over lunch in a quaint café, Rochelle said, "Ivory, I want to thank you for being there for me. I truly don't know what I would've done without you. Thank Tyler for me as well. I'll never forget what you've done for me. I don't have a lot of close friends. I only go out occasionally. But I'm glad I have you for a friend."

Ivory smiled at her kindly. "Things will be okay, Rochelle. You'll see."

"Oh, I know they will be."

"You sound so confident."

"I am, Ivory. I really am. I'm finally convinced of that."

Ivory had chosen her wedding gown. A few alterations had to be made and then it would be delivered to the palazzo. Rochelle helped with the wedding plans. Things were going smoothly and Ivory was looking forward to her wedding day. So was Tyler. She'd never known a man who wanted to get as involved in wedding plans as he did.

Max had gotten his cast and bandages removed and was moving around with only small twinges of pain. That was usually when he overdid it. But Ivory kept an eye on him and made him slow down. He didn't like it but he did as she said most of the time.

One night Ivory, Tyler, and Max went out to dinner. They had a lovely time and laughed a lot. Afterwards they took a stroll, crossing the Rialto Bridge and just looking at the different churches and palazzos. When they got home Tyler went to the library to finish up one last thing on his computer.

Max retired for the evening and Ivory went to her room to get ready for bed. It was after ten o'clock and Tyler would probably be another hour. Once he logged on to his computer he had no notion of time. So Ivory changed and lay down on the sofa. The windows were open and a nice breeze blew in from the water.

Ivory lay there thinking about the wedding and fell asleep. She was having a pleasant dream about Tyler when everything started moving. At first she thought it was an earthquake. Her eyes flew open and she realized that someone was shaking her. Rochelle was looking down at her and saying, "Ivory! Ivory! Wake up! Please!"

Ivory sat up and rubbed her eyes as she said sleepily, "Rochelle?"

"Oh, Ivory! It's happened again! I received another note! This time it was on my bed!"

Ivory was wide-awake now. She looked up at Rochelle. "What did it say?"

"He wants me to meet him in the tower room. He says to bring the jewels with me or I'll be dead by morning!"

"Okay, Rochelle. Take a deep breath. You have to try to remain calm."

"Calm! Are you kidding? How can I remain calm at a time like this? Can we go get the jewels now? I have to be there by midnight. We have to hurry."

"We don't have to go anywhere to get them. Tyler brought them up here several days ago."

"They're here?"

"That's right."

"Then get them. It's almost midnight."

"It is? Where's Tyler? We have to get Tyler."

"I already told him. He said he'd meet us in the tower room."

"But why didn't he come with you? And why didn't he tell you he moved the jewels?"

"Probably because I was hysterical and wouldn't let him get a word in. He's getting a gun from the study."

"A gun?"

"Come on, Ivory!"

"Okay, okay."

She went to Tyler's room and pulled the small oblong box from beneath the bed. Rochelle had followed her. She asked, "The jewels are in there? I thought the box would be larger."

"This is an antique jewel box. It has several layers in it where many pieces of jewelry can be kept. Do I have time to change?"

"No! We can't be late. Tyler is probably on his way there. We can't let him get there before us."

"Okay, Rochelle. Would you please stop being so jumpy? You're making me nervous. You have to keep your wits about you. We're dealing with a cunning murderer."

"I'll try to calm down, but it won't be easy. I've never been so terrified in my life. Oh, Ivory, I don't want to die!"

185

"Hush now. You aren't going to die. Come on, let's go."

The two women left the room and made their way to the fateful tower room, the room where one murder had already been committed. Ivory was trying to be brave, but she was very nervous and frightened. She was going to confront the fiend who'd strangled Abby Ashford. She sincerely hoped Tyler would be there when they arrived.

He'd told her that when the time came he'd wait in the shadows until the murderer showed himself and then he'd take matters into his own hands. On the way up the staircase a thought occurred to Ivory. She spoke in a whisper to Rochelle who was in front of her, "Rochelle! How did he get in? Tyler sealed up all the entrances from the outside."

Rochelle snapped over her shoulder, "How the hell should I know? He's here, that's all I care about."

Ivory said no more because they'd come to the tower room door. Ivory had been carrying the jewel box. Rochelle opened the door and light greeted them. Ivory frowned at this. The last time she'd been in this room there had been no lights. The light switch hadn't worked.

They stepped into the room cautiously and Ivory could see the light source came from candles. Lots of candles. They were lined against the walls in small glass candleholders. Rochelle gasped, "He's been here! Look at all these candles. But it isn't quite midnight yet. We still have a few minutes."

The door closed behind them as they looked around the room. It was empty. Ivory commented, "Tyler isn't here yet."

There was a noise behind them. Turning, Ivory clearly saw part of the wall move inward. They both cried out when a man came into the room. A secret passageway Tyler had missed. The man was wearing a black hooded cloak. In one movement he tossed the hood back and aimed a gun at them. Ivory held her breath. She couldn't believe her eyes. He said, "Tyler won't be coming, Ivory."

She stared in shock at Austin. He said, "He's been

detained."

"Austin!" exclaimed Ivory, "What are you doing?"

"I'm taking what's mine! Now give me the box. I don't want to have to shoot you."

Ivory stared at him for a minute but when he yelled, "Move!" she put the box down and kicked it over to him as she asked, "How could you do this, Austin? *You* of all people? And why?"

"What a stupid question!" he snapped. His whole face seemed to change. "These jewels belong to me!"

The door burst open behind them and Tyler and Julian came in. Tyler was aiming a gun. Julian saw his son. "Austin! What in God's name are you doing? Put that gun down!"

Austin now aimed the gun at Tyler and Julian. "What are you doing here, Father?"

Tyler answered, "We came when we couldn't find Rochelle and Ivory."

Ivory asked, "But didn't Rochelle tell you to meet us here?"

Tyler looked at Rochelle as he replied, "No, I haven't spoken to her all night."

All eyes were on Rochelle. She said, "I thought we could handle it ourselves, Ivory. I'm so sorry I lied to you."

She looked so pitiful Ivory felt a little sorry for her. Julian said angrily, "Never mind that, I want to know why my son is holding a gun on us! Have you lost your mind?"

Austin laughed. "No, Father. I haven't lost my mind. I've come to my senses! Why should Tyler get everything? I don't want to do this, but I have to."

Julian took a step forward and Austin shouted, "Stay where you are! I don't want to kill you like I had to kill Abby!"

Julian gasped. Tyler and Ivory just watched in horror and shock as Julian tried to remain calm. "Austin, you don't know what you're saying. You're sick, son."

"No, I'm not. I had to kill Abby. She wouldn't tell us where the jewels were hidden."

187

Tyler spoke up, "Us? Who is 'us', Austin?"

Austin looked at him and his gun hand began to shake. He snapped, "Never mind!"

Julian said, "You couldn't have thought of all this on your own. You're my son. I know you. Who's behind this, Austin? Who planned all this?"

Austin yelled hysterically, "I did! I planned the whole thing! You don't think I'm clever enough to come up with this, but I am! I am!"

Austin started to cry. He fell to his knees. Julian took another step closer. "Austin, please. Tell me who is behind all this."

Austin looked up at him helplessly. Rochelle spoke from behind Ivory, "I'm behind this, Father."

They all turned to Rochelle. She looked at their faces and laughed. "You were all so easy to fool."

She looked directly at Ivory. "Especially you, Ivory. You really swallowed the whole act, didn't you? Poor pitiful Rochelle needed your help. Needed a friend. I've never needed anyone in my life!"

Ivory stared at Rochelle in numb shock. No! It couldn't be! Julian looked at his daughter as if he were looking at a stranger. "No, Rochelle, it can't be you. I won't accept it, I won't!"

Rochelle looked at her father, shook her head and said angrily, "Well you better accept it, Father. Your little angel concocted this whole diabolical scheme. I overheard Aunt Abby and Victoria talking one day. That's how I found out about the jewels but I didn't find out where they were hidden. Danielle came along and ruined everything. So I decided to devise a plan to scare Abby.

I tampered with her food and even pushed her down the stairs. I wanted her to be terrified of the 'Keeper of the Castle'. The Delegado curse came in quite handy. When she came to this room without the jewels I was outraged. I made Austin kill her. Oh, he didn't want to do it. But I'd talked him into everything else and all it took was my anger to force his hand. Austin is very devoted to me, aren't you brother dear?"

Austin looked at her with fear and terror in his eyes. He held the gun loosely now. Rochelle went on in a menacing tone, "But Austin is weak. He's always needed me. He will always need me."

Ivory asked, "But why, Rochelle? Why have you done all these terrible things?"

Rochelle looked at her and suddenly she had that innocent look on her face again. "For the jewels, dear Ivory. Austin is right. They belong to us, not Tyler."

She then glared at her cousin. "You haven't been here for years, Tyler. You abandoned the family. What right do you have to claim everything?"

Julian spoke up then, "That was my fault. I sent him away because I was afraid he'd be a bad influence on you and Austin. What a joke! Now it appears I sent him away to protect him from you, Rochelle. Look at yourself. You are evil. A murderess!

You murdered your own aunt. Austin may have done your bidding, but you are responsible! How could I have had such a daughter? How could my little girl have done these things? What happened to you?"

She laughed again. "I'll tell you what happened to me, Father. I got smart. You have always underestimated me. You trained Austin to run the family business while you only gave me the simple projects here and there. But I'm the one who is smarter. Smarter than all of you. I should be the one running Ashford Incorporated. Not Austin. Never Austin. It should've been me!

But you never even took the time to notice how intelligent I was. Because I'm a woman you treated me as if I would shatter at any moment. Do you have any idea how insulting that is? After Abby's death Maxwell Lawrence wanted to come here but I couldn't allow that. I'm the one who arranged his accident.

I didn't want anyone here snooping around. I still had to find the jewels. So Austin and I started looking for them. I knew Aunt Vicky knew where they were but Austin refused to harm her. It was the one time he ever stood up to me. He threatened me. Actually threatened me! He told me if I harmed her in any way he'd tell you everything, Father.

I backed down because I needed him. I wanted to get out! Out of this gloomy palazzo and out of Venice. The jewels were my way out. Oh, I promised to take Austin with me but he doesn't really want to go. He likes it here, can you imagine? This place is a tomb. I knew the jewels would bring me freedom at last.

Then Aunt Vicky asked me to go with her to meet Mr. Lawrence. She told me in confidence that Tyler was in Venice. So I went and we brought Tyler and Ivory here. I didn't know they weren't married. Imagine my shock when I found out I'd been fooled. When Aunt Vicky died I knew it was my time to act.

I made up the whole thing about the 'Keeper of the Castle' and I used it again to find out if Ivory or Tyler knew anything about the jewels. To my complete surprise and delight Ivory knew more than I'd ever dreamed. She even knew where they were. After the will was read and I found out Tyler was to get everything except for the measly amount Aunt Vicky had left us, I knew it was time to put my plan into action.

Can't you see, Father? We should get everything, not Tyler! What has he ever done for the company? He isn't entitled to any of it! Nothing! If we get rid of him and Ivory then it will be ours. I know you want that, Father. You worked hard and for what? Seventy-five percent is nothing compared to the whole thing. It can be ours.

Austin doesn't have the stomach to murder, but you can help me. You're strong like I am. We can do this together. Why should you settle for half the jewels and a portion of the company? And this palazzo should belong to you as well. *You* are the one who took care of Abby and Vicky all those years. It's only right that we should have it all.

What's Tyler and Ivory to you? You've hated Tyler until a couple of weeks ago, and Ivory is an outsider. Just someone else in the way of what we want. And her brother will leave once she's gone. We can set up an accident or just make them disappear. I'll leave that up to you. Or maybe it can be the Delegado curse again. Don't you see that this is the only solution? We will be rich. So what do you say, Father? Will you join Austin and me in this? Will you help us? We're only taking what is rightfully ours, after all. Once they're out of the way it will be so wonderful. I can travel and you can run everything just like you always have, only now it will all be yours. Come on, Father, help me get rid of them. When you take a life once, the next time is easy. And think what we'll gain. We'll have everything at last."

Chapter Thirty Two

Julian stared at his once beautiful daughter in shock and horror and a little disbelief. He could almost believe this was all a bad dream. No, a nightmare. A nightmare of his worst imagining. But it wasn't a dream. It was all so very real and his children, whom he'd always cared for and loved, had turned into vicious monsters. Especially Rochelle.

Austin was looking at his sister in fear now. He hadn't moved. Tyler and Ivory looked at Rochelle in disbelief also. Julian ran a hand through his silver hair and then looked at his daughter again. "You are insane, Rochelle. How could you think I would even consider helping you? I've always taught you the difference between right and wrong.

But you have no morals, no ethics. You've taken a life and you want to take two more with my help. And look what you've done to your brother. You made him kill his own aunt. It isn't right to take something that doesn't belong to you, something that you haven't rightfully earned.

Vicky left her estate to Tyler because she loved him. It was her decision to make, not yours. Tyler is my nephew and in spite of the past I would now protect him and Ivory with my life."

Rochelle pulled out a gun and said, "Then give your life for them, Father."

She pulled the trigger and the sound of the gun ricocheted around the room. Ivory cried out and Julian fell. Quickly, Rochelle picked up the jewel box and made her way to the secret panel as she said, "I gave you a chance, Father."

Ivory went to Julian and Tyler aimed his gun at Rochelle. She looked at him and said, "Don't, Tyler. I'll kill Ivory, I swear I will."

She aimed at Ivory and Tyler knew she would pull the trigger. He angrily snapped, "How did you get to be such an evil bitch?"

At first she seemed caught off guard by his remark. The she laughed and said, "A bitch I might be, but I'm a rich bitch!"

She took aim at Ivory. "Stop, Rochelle!" Austin suddenly exclaimed.

She looked at her brother with a frown marring her brow. He had his gun aimed at her. She'd all but forgotten he had one. She laughed again. "Come on, Austin. We both know you haven't got the guts to pull the trigger."

"You shouldn't have shot father. This has to stop. He's right. You are evil. You're a monster!"

"Put the gun down, Austin, before you hurt yourself. Do you think I won't kill you? You all make me sick! You and your happy little family. You are all disgusting!"

She turned the gun on her brother then but Austin pulled the trigger first. Another deafening sound vibrated through the room and Rochelle cried out and dropped the gun to put her hand to her side where blood was soaking her pale yellow dress. She almost dropped the jewel box but managed to hang on to it.

She looked at her brother in disbelief. "You shot me! How could you, Austin? You love me. You need me. Look what you've done, you idiot!"

Austin appeared to be surprised by his actions also. Rochelle cried out, "I'll get you for this! The 'Keeper of the Castle' will return! I'll kill every last one of you!"

She ran through the passageway then. Julian said through his pain, "Go after her!"

Tyler bent down beside his uncle and asked Ivory, "How bad is he?"

"It looks like the bullet went through his side. He needs a doctor."

"Call one. I'm going after Rochelle."

He ran through the passageway then and Austin crawled over to his father. "I'm so sorry, Father. I didn't think she'd shoot you. I had to stop her."

"I know you did. I'll be okay, Austin."

"Are you sure? You're bleeding badly."

Ivory stood up. "I'll go call the doctor. Stay with your father, Austin."

Austin looked up at her. "You trust me, Ivory? When you know I've killed Aunt Abby?"

"You didn't exactly do it all by yourself, now did you? I think you are a very mixed up young man, Austin. But I also think you care about your father, now stay here while I go call the doctor."

She left and Austin looked down at his father. But Julian had passed out.

Tyler was a little ways behind Rochelle. She'd previously lit candles in the narrow passageway as well. He knew there was no way out because he'd boarded up all the secret panels to the outside. So she would try to get out another way. Tyler didn't have to wonder about it for long. There were droplets of blood on the cold stone floor and on the walls here and there.

All he had to do was follow the trail. He followed her down narrow steps to the first floor and then out through the dining room to the back entrance of the palazzo. He found her outside on the dock, looking for a gondola anxiously. Apparently she hadn't planned on such a sudden escape or she would have arranged for a boat to be waiting.

Her plan had been to murder him and Ivory and leave it at that. There had been no reason for her to leave the palazzo at all this night. But things hadn't gone according to plan and she was standing there alone, in a pool of her own blood getting more desperate by the moment. She didn't even have a gun any longer. She'd dropped it when Austin had unexpectedly shot her.

"Rochelle!"

She spun around. There was blood all over the front of her dress now, and some of it started to run down her legs. She looked pale. "Stay away, Tyler!"

"Give it up, Rochelle. You're hurt. It's all over."

"No it isn't! I haven't come this far to give up now!"

"You've lost too much blood. Come back and we'll get a doctor."

She laughed. "So you can have the jewels? Never!"

"Forget the jewels! Do you want to die?"

As he spoke she fell to one knee, the loss of blood making her dizzy. She looked around. For once there were no gondolas within sight. She spoke, her voice weakening, "Isn't this odd? I've never seen such a night as this. Usually there's half a dozen gondolas' out here. I know because I've watched them since I was a child. It seems that God himself is conspiring against me."

She turned to Tyler then and she seemed calmer. "I'll never let you have these jewels, Tyler. They're mine! They're going to get me out of here and make my life fun for a change!"

"Rochelle, can't you see that you won't be able to go anywhere in your condition?"

She doubled over at the pain but wouldn't release her grasp on the box. She looked up at him through her blonde curls and said, "You'll never get the jewels, Tyler. Never! Never! Never!"

And then she threw the box as far as she could over the water. The box splashed and then slowly sunk. Rochelle fell on her back, still trying to stop the flow of blood with her hand.

She laughed then and Tyler thought it an unnatural sound. He went to her. She pushed her hair out of her eyes, leaving blood smears on her white face and hair. She stopped laughing to look up at him. "Told you you'd never get the jewels. Centuries of Venice are under that water. You'll never find them."

She squeezed her eyes shut as pain overwhelmed her. Tyler got down beside her. "Rochelle, you little fool. I would've given you the damn jewels. Don't you know that?"

She coughed up blood and wiped it away with her hand as she spoke in a mere whisper, "Now you tell me."

"I'll go get a doctor."

"No!"

She reached for his hand. "Don't leave me. I have to tell you something."

He leaned over to hear her words. She spoke in a choked voice, "I always liked Ivory. It's so odd. I was going to kill her. But she really wanted to help me. No one ever wanted to help me."

And then the life went entirely out of her. Her arms fell lifeless on the deck and Tyler felt her pulse. Rochelle was dead. He had witnessed the second death of a family member.

Chapter Thirty Three

The doctor had come and seen to Julian's injury. The bullet had gone clean through as Ivory had predicted and Julian would be fine. The doctor ordered him to stay in bed. The police had arrived and Max had come out of his room in his pajamas to see what all the fuss was about. He was as shocked as everyone else had been when Ivory told him all that Rochelle had done with her brother's help.

Austin was taken away and Tyler thought he'd probably wind up in a mental institution until he was better. How much time he'd spend in jail or an institution for his part in Rochelle's schemes was unknown. Julian had been given pain pills so he could sleep. Tyler and Ivory stayed with him until he finally dozed off. Before he did he said, "I'll be here for Austin when he gets out of jail. No matter how long it takes."

Ivory and Tyler went to their rooms in silence and once they lay in bed together Tyler told her what Rochelle had said just before she died. After awhile he said, "I don't know if I can live here now. So much has happened. Maybe the palazzo is really cursed."

Ivory didn't say anything for awhile and then she held him close and suggested, "Maybe we can get away for a few weeks. After we're married we can go on a honeymoon. Do you still want to be married here?"

"I don't know. It depends on how Julian feels about it. He's sure been through hell."

"Yes. In fact, we all have."

"It's all over now, baby. Maybe a wedding is just what this place needs."

"Perhaps. But I keep seeing it all over again in my head."

"Me too. I never suspected Rochelle."

"Of course you didn't. It took all of us by complete surprise. I keep remembering her and Austin on our

197

sightseeing trip. They were so helpful and knowledgeable about each place we went. And we all had so much fun that day. Austin had us laughing constantly and both of them seemed pleased to show me around.

And the other day when Rochelle and I went shopping for my wedding gown she told me how much she appreciated my help. How she was glad we were friends."

"The whole thing is unbelievable."

Ivory was momentarily quiet. Tyler muttered, "Such a waste."

After another lapse of silence Ivory said, "The jewels are gone now. They're at the bottom of all that water."

"No, they aren't."

Ivory looked up at him in surprise and then frowned. "What do you mean? You told me Rochelle threw them way out in the water and they sank."

"She did. But those weren't the real jewels. I put rocks in the jewel box."

Ivory gasped, shocked once more. Tyler smiled down at her. "I had no intention of giving the Ashford jewels to anyone."

"My God, Tyler! You took such a chance!"

"Sure I did. But those gems belonged to my grandmother. I was going to sell my half but maybe now I'll keep them. There are some exquisite pieces. I want to give some of them to you."

"I'll accept one or two pieces, but sell the rest. Those damn stones have caused too much heartache."

"It wasn't the stones themselves, baby. It was Rochelle's greed."

"Whatever."

"Okay. Maybe you're right."

"I know I am."

The palazzo was gloomy and they all attended yet another funeral at the same cemetery. Austin wasn't with them this time and Julian had to take it slow because of his

198

injury. A priest or minister spoke no kind words. They just watched as her white coffin was lowered into the earth. What was there to really say?

Julian specifically asked that no priest be present. It was an odd funeral. No one was there but them. Ivory guessed that it was a fitting funeral for a murderess, but she couldn't help but remember Rochelle as she had been before the incident in the tower room. She wondered if everything had been an act.

Rochelle had told Tyler that she'd liked her. But she had still planned on murdering her. Abby must have been so shocked to find Austin and Rochelle in the tower room. She probably had been completely fooled. Rochelle had done a superb acting job. And now here she was, being lowered into the ground.

What Rochelle had pretended to fear had really happened. Julian hadn't mentioned his daughter once since that horrible night. He was probably still in shock. Ivory felt sorry for him. He'd lost both his children. She remembered when Tyler had been so convinced that Julian had murdered his sister.

How very wrong he had been. Julian had been shocked to the core when his daughter had asked him to help her kill them. Even if he and Tyler hadn't made amends with each other, she was sure Julian would never have agreed to such a thing. How strange things had worked out. Not so very long ago Austin and Rochelle were part of their lives.

They had been family and friends. Now Rochelle was dead, Austin had been taken away by the police, and the man whom Tyler had never trusted was now his only family as well as his friend. It was very strange how life turned out sometimes. Very strange.

No one lingered at Rochelle's grave. They all turned and walked away without a backward glance. Ivory glanced over at Julian and found him frowning. Was he remembering Rochelle as a little girl? There was nothing anyone could say or do to help him. Tyler was deep in thought as well.

She knew he partially blamed himself. She knew him so very well now. Was he regretting ever returning to Venice? But if he hadn't, his grandmother would have died without ever seeing him again. Besides, Tyler and her would have never fallen in love. There was really no use in speculating on 'what ifs' and 'maybes'.

Ivory had often been told that she thought too much. It was usually her brother who told her this. She looked over at him now. He was the only one who wasn't scowling. He wasn't exactly smiling, but he wasn't as tormented as the rest of the funeral party. Good ole' Max. Nothing seemed to faze him.

Rochelle and Austin's presence was missed at the dinner table. Three days after burying her, Julian showed up for dinner. The silence stretched on but no one wanted to attempt polite conversation. They all started when Max slapped his fork down and said, "That's it! I can't stand this silence anymore! Somebody say something! Don't we have a wedding to talk about?"

Julian looked over at him. Max smiled, bowed his head and said, "Sorry. I guess it's really none of my business."

Julian said, "No, Max is right. It's time to put the past behind us. I know we've all been through a lot but we have to find a way to go on. I think the wedding should proceed as planned."

Tyler looked over at his uncle. "Are you sure? We don't have to have it now. We can postpone it."

"No, Tyler." Julian told him, "I don't want you to postpone the wedding. I'm finished with grieving and feeling sorry for myself. Dwelling on things isn't going to change them. It does none of us any good."

Ivory smiled at him. "You are quite a man, Julian Ashford."

He smiled back at her. They resumed eating but the atmosphere was lighter. Julian pushed his plate away and asked Max, "Did you know your sister plays chess extremely well? She beat me several times."

"Of course I know," replied Max with a grin, "I taught her how to play."

Julian laughed. "So you're the one I have to thank for losing a hundred bucks!"

"I'm afraid so."

"Tell me, Maxwell, would you care to play a game later?"

Max's face lit up. "Of course I would."

"Marvelous."

Things improved. The palazzo was no longer such a maudlin place. As the wedding drew nearer Tyler and Ivory thought of nothing else. When the day finally arrived they were very happy. Ivory wore a beautiful white lace and satin gown with a Spanish lace veil. Julian gave the bride away and Max was Best Man. Mr. Darius attended as well as Danielle and the austere looking cook.

When Tyler kissed the bride everyone clapped and offered congratulations. Afterwards the newlywed couple spent their wedding night at the palazzo. The next day Julian gave them a wedding present; two round trip tickets to Munich, Germany as well as their hotel stay.

They were very pleased and excited. Neither one of them had ever been to Germany. They left the next day. They liked it so much they stayed an extra two weeks. Germany was beautiful and they had the time of their lives. Ivory never wanted to leave but knew Tyler needed to get back for business reasons.

While they were away Max and Julian became fast friends. They played chess almost every night and Max even convinced the distinguished gentleman to go out twice a week. Julian enjoyed showing Max the sights. And Max loved it. A whole new Venice opened up for him. Julian started to change. He became more outgoing, spending more time away from the palazzo.

He'd even taken to reading Max's novels. He found

them in a bookstore and Max was pleased when he caught him reading one night. Caught in the act, Julian grinned and said, "Your books are very good, Max ole' boy. Riveting and very professionally done. I've enjoyed each one immensely."

"Good grief, Julian. How many have you read?"

"All of them. This is the last one."

"Really? I'm honored."

"And so you should be. I usually only read books on improving profits in one's business. But I find these fascinating. Are you working on another one?"

"Yes. I just finished one."

"Good. I can hardly wait to read it."

"Wow. You really *do* like my work."

"That's what I just said. You want to go out for a drink?"

"Again?"

"Of course. This is all your fault, you know."

"What did I do now?"

"You changed the way I live. I used to be content just shutting myself up in this palazzo. Now I actually look forward to going out."

"Glad to hear it. You needed to get out and enjoy life a little."

"So you want to go?"

Max laughed. "You lead the way, ole' man."

Chapter Thirty Four

When Ivory and Tyler returned to the palazzo they were welcomed with open arms. Max had missed his sister and best friend very much. After one day they noticed the change in Julian. Ivory and Tyler were having dinner and were wondering where Max and Julian were when the two men in question walked in.

They were both in black suits. Tyler asked in a tone of surprise, "Are you two going somewhere?"

Julian straightened his black silk tie and replied, "Yes, we're going dancing. Want to come along?"

Ivory nearly choked on her food. Tyler patted her on the back as he tried not to smile. He replied, "No, thank you, Uncle Julian. I have work to do. Tell me, do you two do this often? Go out, I mean?"

Max ran a hand through his dark hair. "Sure we do. Two or three times a week."

They just stared as the two handsome men left and then looked at one another. Ivory found her voice first, "I don't believe it! Did you see that?"

"I sure did. My uncle never goes anywhere. Especially not dancing. What's happened around here?"

"I don't know but let's go with them next time."

"We will. This I have to see for myself."

Ivory and Tyler went out with Max and Julian a few times and each time they really enjoyed themselves. Julian even mentioned throwing a party at the palazzo. Both men had made a few new friends and wanted to show them where they lived. But what really shocked them was when Julian told Ivory she had a very talented brother.

He told them he'd read all his books and really liked them. The change in Julian was a surprise. But quite a pleasant one. He was happy now. One day when Max and

Julian were in the library playing chess, Ivory walked in and Max was saying, "You can't move there, Julian."

"Of course I can."

"Well, you *can*, but if you do you'll be in serious trouble."

Julian frowned at him and then at the chessboard. Ivory said, "Listen! I have news. Something's happened!"

Tyler came in behind her and put his arm around her waist. Max didn't look up as he said with a sigh, "What now?"

"I'm pregnant!"

Both men looked up at them then. Julian smiled. "That's wonderful, Ivory, Tyler."

He looked at Max and said, "Don't just sit there, Maxwell. Say something to your sister!"

"I'm just so surprised!"

Ivory beamed at them. Max asked, "Does this mean we'll be hearing a baby cry at all hours?"

Julian slammed his pawn down. "What a thing to say, Max! A baby is just what this place needs. And I can baby-sit. I love babies."

"Well, so do I!" interrupted Max, "I will especially love Tyler and Ivory's baby. And who says *you're* going to baby-sit? *I* should baby-sit my nephew."

"What!" exclaimed Julian, "A minute ago you were complaining about the baby crying. Now you want to baby-sit?"

"Of course I do. I will make a wonderful babysitter."

"What makes you think that?" asked Julian, "You told me how you travel all over. The poor thing won't even recognize you. It would be better if *I* watch the child."

"No, it wouldn't. I'm not going to be traveling as much."

"Sure. You say that now. But will you then? That's the question."

They both turned to Ivory and Tyler, who were watching them in disbelief. Tyler said, "Gentlemen, the baby isn't even here yet."

Max asked, "But when it is here, can I baby-sit? I've always wanted to."

Julian put in, "And me, Tyler? I'm very good with babies. You'll need an experienced person."

Max glared at Julian. "What do you mean by that? Just because I've never done it before doesn't mean I won't be good at it."

He turned to Ivory and Tyler. "What do you say? Can I do it?"

"And can I?" asked Julian. Tyler and Ivory looked at one another and then at the two waiting men and said in unison, "Whatever."

The palazzo seemed to shake with the laughter that followed.

The End

Printed in Great Britain
by Amazon

41651407R00126